The Awakening of Dan Hanley

A Novel

By

Rita K. Hamilton

authorHOUSE

1663 LIBERTY DRIVE, SUITE 200
BLOOMINGTON, INDIANA 47403
(800) 839-8640
www.authorhouse.com

This book is a work of fiction. Places, events, and situations in this story are purely fictional and any resemblance to actual persons, living or dead, is coincidental.

© 2004 Rita K. Hamilton.
All Rights Reserved.

No part of this book may be reproduced, stored in a retrieval system, or transmitted by any means without the written permission of the author.

Cover by DeAnna L. Cannon

First published by AuthorHouse 08/12/04

ISBN: 1-4184-6959-9 (sc)

Library of Congress Control Number: 2004094182

Printed in the United States of America
Bloomington, Indiana

This book is printed on acid-free paper.

Dedicated to my husband, Howard. Without his support I would never have the courage to pursue my dream.

CHAPTER ONE

Though it was still too early, Dan paced the living room, waiting for his friend Bob to pick him up. He groaned inwardly as he heard his mother emerge from her bedroom, where she had secluded herself after seeing his father and younger brothers off to work and play. He turned. She was hiding something behind her back.

She straightened her shoulders. "Going to college *will* change you," she pronounced.

He halted beside his boxes and secondhand suitcases. Squaring his shoulders, he steeled himself for another argument.

With a new look of determination, she pulled the worn family Bible from behind her back. "Through all the years since you quit," she said, "I've comforted myself with the thought you would someday return to my church. That's because I know you are still basically a good Christian boy. But you won't stay that way if college corrupts you like it did the Bradfords' two girls and Mary Kelly's boy."

"Mom, you're worried about nothing. I'm not anything like Brad Kelly. Even if I was, I won't have the time or the money for loose girls and wild parties the way he did. And your teachings are too ingrained in me for me to turn atheistic like the Bradford girls. I guarantee you, I won't change that much."

"I know you believe that, Son; but it would ease my mind a great deal if you would swear on your great-grandmother's Bible that you won't let going to college change you. I know you. Once you've sworn to something, you'll do your uppermost to keep your word."

He swore, with every intention of keeping his promise.

Early afternoon of the same day, an old yellow cat watched from the doorway as Dan plopped the last of his suitcases down on the blue-patterned carpet. Purposely ignoring the feline, Dan turned slowly, absorbing the homey atmosphere of Mrs. Canfield's spare bedroom. Having been willing to settle for anything, he was delighted with what he had been offered. The homemade, light blue bedspread, matching curtains, and entire room were impeccable like his new landlady—an unknown, distant cousin of his father.

His brown eyes scanned the aged desk; two glass-fronted bookcases that Mrs. Canfield had emptied for him; and the three-piece, maple bedroom suite that looked as if it had squatted in the same spot for thirty years. He bounced his rear up and down on the mattress. It was softer than he liked, but acceptable.

With trained eye, he checked out the large, old school teacher's desk. Even it suited his needs perfectly. He ran his fingers lightly over the top, noting that it needed refinishing. Maybe that would be one of his jobs while he is here.

A gentle breeze tickled the back of his neck, drawing his attention to an open window near the bed. The second story window overlooked Mrs. Canfield's backyard. A chain-link fence enclosed the yard and ended against the sides of her one-and-half car garage, which faced the alley.

Katy, one of Mrs. Canfield's gray cats, sunned herself, belly-up, on the walk leading to the back gate. The second gray cat, Princess, romped near a pink rosebush. The two cats were distinguishable, even from Dan's position, by the white patch on Princess' head.

Taylor, the yellow cat that had followed Dan upstairs, still sat in the doorway watching him. Dan frowned. He disliked cats, but was determined to put up with these three.

Staring out the window, he remembered how hopeless he had felt when he had sent out inquiries through everyone he knew, and some that he met for the first time. He had figured the odds of finding someone living within commuting distance of the university lay on the miraculous level. Not normally a prayer, he mumbled, "Please, help me stay in Mrs. Canfield's good graces."

Princess leaped at an insect hidden in the grass, causing Dan to note how tall and full of dandelions the yard was. He smiled. This could be his chance to start earning his keep. His gaze shifted to the boxes and suitcases waiting on the carpet, then back to the yard, and back to the suitcases. Unpacking could wait.

Dan skirted around Taylor and hurried down the stairs. Barely avoiding colliding with the birdcage standing in the hallway, he darted into the home's only fully modernized room—the kitchen. Mrs. Canfield sat at the table, sipping a freshly poured cup of tea.

Dan blurted out, "Where's your lawnmower? I want to cut the grass." Remembering his manners, he added in as respectable a tone as he could muster, "If that's all right with you of course."

An uneasy look flitted across her refine, pink features. "That can wait." She smiled nervously. "I'm glad you're here. Please sit down. We need to talk."

Alarmed, Dan sank into a chair. Was she going to sit down a bunch of rules? He had worried that she would want to treat him like an irresponsible teen-ager, giving him a horde of do's and don'ts', what and what nots' to follow. After all he had just turned twenty-one. He could not stand it if she tried to treat him the way his parents did.

He had continued to live at home after high school in order to save money. And, even though he had worked full-time and contributed his share, there had been several stormy sessions because his parents persisted in treating him like a minor. He stared at Mrs. Canfield, waiting with dread to see what she was going to do.

"Would you like something to drink? I've stocked up on soft drinks for you."

"No, thank you."

Mrs. Canfield sipped her tea slowly and studied him over the rim of her cup. She took note of his slender, well-shaped build; heavy stock of chestnut hair; fair skin, and thick, dark eyebrows that gave him the appearance of continual brooding. A nice-looking young man, she thought, in spite of a nose slightly too wide for his features. She took a deep breath, calmed her mind to an alpha brain-wave level, and stared into his vivid brown eyes in an attempt to seek insight into his character. He glanced down in embarrassment. Still unsure of himself as a man, and too strait-laced, she concluded. This could get touchy.

She shifted her eyes heavenward and silently prayed. "Lord, give me the right words." Her penetrating, gray-green eyes returned to Dan. "What do you know about me?"

She had thrown him off guard. "Wha--What?"

"What do you know about me?"

"Only--only what you wrote." He tried to regain his composure as he pulled a paper out of his wallet. Unfolding a letter tattered from many re-readings, he scanned what he already knew by heart.

Dear Dan:
I learned, through mutual relatives, of your desire to attend college here. I am a housewife, soon to be seventy, and live within walking distance of the university.

I understand you were thoroughly trained as a handyman by your versatile and highly skilled father. It would please me greatly to work out a room and board arrangement with you. I own a small, century-old, two-story house that is in constant need of repairs, most of which are too much for me. My husband, Robert, always handled such matters before. He died of a heart attack four years ago. He was a professor of philosophy at the university until he retired. Our only child, a son, lives two thousand miles away in California.

My husband's pension, combined with some wisely made investments, has made me reasonably comfortable financially. As a result, I do not need a cash-paying renter nearly as much as I need an in-house handyman. I live with three cats and a parakeet, and hope to get a dog soon. If you do not mind the animals, I am willing to give it a try. I am confident we can work out an arrangement satisfactory to us both.

Sincerely yours,
Margaret Jean Canfield

Finding no hint in the letter as to the meaning behind her question, a puzzled Dan glanced at his landlady.

She lifted a quizzical, well-shaped eyebrow and pointed to the paper in his hand. "No one has told you anything else?"

"No."

She sighed. "I was afraid of that. Your father's family always did pretend my gift didn't exist."

"Gift?"

"Yes. That's what we need to discuss," she said with a hint of nervousness. Deciding flattery would help in easing into it, she added, "Being an up-to-date and well-read young man, I'm sure you are aware of the work being done in the field of psychic research. Many educated people now acknowledge the reality of extrasensory perception."

Pleased by her description of himself, Dan nodded in agreement. He saw no reason for marring her image of him by admitting he seldom read anything except his home county newspaper. As for the psychic, he vaguely recalled his mother referring to it as the work of the devil. He started to chuckle at the idea of anyone taking such nonsense seriously when he noticed Mrs. Canfield's solemn expression. He stiffened.

She traced and retraced the rim of her teacup with a finger. "I'm sure you're aware there are many forms of ESP: psychokinesis, precognition, clairvoyance, and telepathy to name a few."

He waved nonchalantly, and lied. "Of course."

"Well." She took a deep breath. "I have a rather unusual psychic gift."

"You do?" Figuring he had better humor her, he asked, "What kind?"

"I can participate in two-way communication with animals."

"W--wh--what?"

"I can communicate psychically with animals, mainly cats and dogs."

Dan sat dumbfounded. What he was seeing and what he was hearing didn't compute. For her age, Mrs. Canfield was a beauty. He noted her correct posture;

slender, stylish clothed figure; and silver-gray, beauty shop hair-do. Only a thin upper lip that disappears when she smiles deeply and slightly pudgy cheeks detracted from her appearance. In every way she appeared the perfect example of a lady from her generation. She even looked queen-like at times. She just didn't seem the weirdo type.

"You needed to know, Dan, because people often consult me about problems with their pets. I also do a lot of volunteer work for a private shelter for homeless animals. If the need should arise, I would like to feel I could call on you for help."

As he continued to gawk at her, the image of his always on guard against sin, Bible-quoting mother flashed through his mind. Could she be right after all? Was it really possible for someone to be given evil powers? Was this attractive, old woman, who had offered him the opportunity of a lifetime, a witch? No, he couldn't believe that. But, if she wasn't, then she was lying for some unknown reason and that could still spell trouble.

Confronted with something he didn't know how to handle, Dan felt the urge to withdraw. He jumped up, grabbing his chair to keep it from falling. "I--I've got to think about this." Ignoring her expression pleading for understanding, he hurried out of kitchen and house.

Not knowing where else to go, he wandered toward the university and sank down against a maple tree at the core of the empty campus. He pondered his predicament. What was he getting himself into? Was Mrs. Canfield evil, a shyster, or just plain crazy? He wished he knew which of the three it was. Then maybe he would know how to respond to her.

As if searching for the answer, he glanced around at the small park-like area populated by a variety of trees native to Indiana. Empty sidewalks crisscrossed it. Squirrels chatted and played in the branches above his head. He relaxed against the tree, appreciating the park's serenity and protection from the sun. This was his favorite place on campus. It's naturalness made a stark contrast to the sterile outer edges of the university. There, out of Dan's sight, were the large, shadeless parking lots, multistory classrooms, and modern dormitories. Some were closed until fall. Others, like Dan, waited for the start of summer classes in two days.

While the buildings seemed willing to wait an eternity, Dan was anxious to begin. Because of his late start, he didn't want to spend one second longer than necessary getting his degree. He planned to complete four years in three, starting with this summer session.

He closed his eyes and tapped the back of his head against the tree trunk. Why? Oh why, hadn't he tried to make better grades in high school? And why had his ex-friend stolen his identity and ruined his credit? He knew something that all the school and bank officials who had turned him down didn't. He had enough determination to do it. At least Kyle State University had been willing to accept him on probation.

If Mrs. Canfield hadn't made her offer, he would have had to either give up entirely or complete his education piecemeal over many years while he worked full-time. He knew he didn't have the patience for the latter and the thought of doing the first overwhelmed him with despair.

The yapping of a small dog distracted him. He opened his eyes. A fox terrier was barking at a squirrel it had chased up a nearby oak. Dan frowned. Animals! Why had Mrs. Canfield turned out to be such a kook? Or worse? Her invitation had seemed so perfect. Even the nearness of her home to the university appeared heaven arranged. It had enabled him to sell his car and add the money to his savings, giving him just enough to cover books and tuition for the whole three years.

He scowled at the still yapping terrier. Grabbing a stick, Dan threw it at the dog. "Go away!"

He leaned back against the maple and closed his eyes. What if living with Mrs. Canfield became an embarrassment? Or worse? Mr. Talbert had drilled into him that a man needed to maintain an above reproach reputation in order to build a good business with repeat customers. It was certain associating with Mrs. Canfield couldn't help his reputation.

And what about his parents? For the first time, he was glad they disapproved of his going to college. There was little chance they would visit him here and find out about her. He recalled the conversation he had with his mother that morning.

He had made her a promise. And he intended to keep it. He wasn't going to let Mrs. Canfield, or anyone else, influence him into breaking it. Still, he knew he would be in trouble with his mother for sure if she ever heard about Mrs. Canfield's claim. She would never give him any peace until he quit school.

As if fearing they were in danger of disappearing, he glanced around at the nearest buildings waiting to help him fulfill his dreams. Surrounding the park on all sides, they were the oldest structures on campus. Ivy-covered and Tudor Gothic in style, they reminded him of great barriers keeping the sterile, but functional outer campus from encroaching on the living, peace restoring center where he sat. Suddenly he sat straight up. That's what he needed. A plan of action that would serve as a form of protection for him in the same way those old buildings seemed to protect the park.

Dan felt something paw his leg. The fox terrier dropped the stick, cocked his head, and waited eagerly for Dan to throw it again. Dan laughed and gave in. He petted the dog. It twisted with delight.

Forming his resolve as he talked, Dan confided to the terrier. "There is no choice. I'll have to stick it out, at least until another solution appears. Meanwhile I'll make absolutely certain that I never let it slip when I'm home on vacations. My parents have somehow managed to live in the dark all these years without ever having heard of my Dad's distant cousin's peculiarities. I'm going to do my best to make sure it stays that way.

"Then, just to be safe, I'm going to keep as much distance between Mrs. Canfield and myself as is humanly possible under the circumstances. Without offending her to the place she'd kick me out, of course. It'll be a strict, business-only arrangement or I'm out the door." The dog wagged its stubby tail. Spying a squirrel, it yapped, and took chase.

Dan marched back to Mrs. Canfield's. She was sweeping the front porch. The closer he approached, the more vigorous she swept. He hiked up the steps and stopped in front of her. She halted and gave him a troubled, questioning look. He straightened into what he hoped was a businesslike stance. "I'll cut the grass now and unpack after supper. If that's okay with you?"

She smiled so broadly her upper lip disappeared. "That's fine."

He nodded curtly. "Good."

She hummed "Bringing in the Sheaves" as he headed around the house to the garage to get the lawnmower.

The next morning when the first rays of daylight filtered into Dan's room he leaped out of bed, anxious to prove he was worth his keep. Skipping breakfast, he gulped down some coffee and set to work removing the outer aluminum storm windows so he could paint the wood around the inside windows. Using an extension ladder, he scraped off the pealing white paint and puttied the upstairs windows in preparation for painting. Then he switched to a stepladder for the ground story windows. He was in the process of positioning the ladder under the first window when he sensed someone watching him.

A girl, around nineteen, stood with her hands behind her back. She flashed him a friendly smile. "Hi."

Dan smiled back shyly. With only two younger brothers and no sisters, he had never learned to be comfortable around girls. Tongue-tied, he took in her rosy skin, small round nose, and ash brown hair, cut stylishly short. She wasn't the classic beauty type like Mrs. Canfield. Her build was too average and hippy. But she was sure cute. She had the deepest dimples he'd ever seen.

"I'm Laurie Kay Carpenter. I live there." She pointed toward the yellow house next door. Her dark eyes sparkled. "You must be Dan. I heard you were coming."

He swallowed and nodded. Yearning for something clever to say, he could only stare. He regretted not having taken time to shave and was acutely aware of his paint-stained work clothes. He wondered how he appeared to her. He often worried his slender 5'11" frame didn't look masculine enough to girls.

Laurie pointed to the ladder he still clutched. "I hope I'm not interfering with your work."

The mention of work brought Dan out of his trance. He had hoped to get as much done as possible that day, since summer classes started tomorrow. "That's okay. I can work while we talk." He finished arranging the ladder under the window and started scraping vigorously while probing his brain for something to say.

Laurie studied him. Liking what she saw, she asked, "Where are you from?"

"Gellettsburg."

"I never heard of it."

"That doesn't surprise me. It is a hundred miles south of here and only has a population of about one thousand. Have you lived here all your life?"

"That's right. I work at Indian State Park in the summer. But, I'll be a sophomore at the university when classes start this fall. Maybe we could walk back and forth to campus and eat lunch at the student center together when our schedules permit."

Dan nearly dropped his scraper from surprise. He suddenly wished he'd had the courage to date more often in high school. Then maybe he would've known how to react to her without blushing. Gathering up his courage, he mumbled, "It might be nice to have someone to walk with on occasion."

"What did you say?"

His face reddened more. "It would be nice to have someone to walk with."

"Good. It's settled." For several silent minutes she watched him while he pretended to concentrate on his scraping. She started to ask him a question a couple of times, but kept hesitating. Finally her curiosity overpowered her. "I hope I'm not being too nosy. You don't have to tell me if you don't want."

"What is it?"

"Well, I can't help wondering. Aren't you a little old for a freshman?"

"I hadn't planned on going to college. After I graduated from high school, I went to work on the maintenance crew of a plastics molding company in the next town."

"What made you change your mind?"

"Mr. Talbert, the big boss. Sometimes my job took me into the front office. The work they did there began to intrigue me. Mr. Talbert noticed and explained a lot. The more I learned, the more I wanted to be on the business end of things, either in sales or personnel."

His shyness disappeared as he warmed up to his favorite subject. "I want to be the one giving orders instead of taking them all the time. I want people to look up to me the way they look up to Mr. Talbert. I want to prove to my parents that I can be somebody. When I told Mr. Talbert I wanted to be a businessman like him, he said I needed a college education. So I started saving money as fast as I could. And here I am."

"Are your parents helping you with expenses?"

Dan snorted. "No. My mother is angry with Mr. Talbert for filling me with worldly ideas. She's afraid I'll be corrupted by 'godless professors' as she calls them. My father believes any book learning over and above the basic is a waste of time for people like us. He said he wouldn't stand in my way, but he wouldn't help either."

"Oh." Laurie said sympathetically, "I see." She smiled. "I'm glad they couldn't discourage you from coming. You're majoring in business administration then?"

"That's right. I haven't picked a minor yet. It'll be either marketing or computer science. Mr. Talbert said either one could help in getting a job."

Laurie nodded in agreement and fell silent. Dan watched her out of the corner of his eye while he scraped a window frame. He asked, "Why are you going to college?"

"I want to be a home economics teacher. My minor is religious studies."

Dan stopped and stared at her. "Isn't that a strange combination?"

She sighed. "That's what everybody says. But it doesn't seem so strange to me." She added defensively, "I picked home economics for a career, and religious studies for my own edification. I believe studying the tenets of all religions, Christian and non-Christian, helps a person to grow spiritually. I want to build upon a relationship with an all encompassing God, that isn't limiting because of some manmade dogmas of a particular group."

Dan couldn't help gawking at her. Was she speaking heresy?

They were distracted by someone shouting, "Laurie!" from the yard of a gray house across the street. A big, blonde man, about Dan's age, crossed over to them. He smiled warmly at Laurie. "There's a dance Friday night out at the fairgrounds. Would you go with me?"

Laurie's whole countenance turned icy. "Bill, I've told you a hundred times. I won't go out with you. Why can't you leave it at that?"

Bill hung his head like a huge puppy being scolded. "I keep hoping that one of these days you'll realize I ain't so bad and go with me."

In a chilling voice, tinged with anger, she said, "There is nothing you can do or say that will ever cause me to change my mind. So just leave me alone."

The big man wilted. Dan couldn't help feeling sorry for him. Laurie had been down right rude. Then Bill spied him watching from the ladder. He straightened his brawny frame, his expression taking on the look of a bully. "Who are you?"

Dan leaned down and extended his hand. "Dan Hanley. I'm rooming here while I attend classes at the university."

Bill ignored Dan's outstretched hand. Recognizing a potential rival when he saw one and embarrassed that Dan had witnessed his rejection, he snorted. "A college snob. I should've known. You're the type Laurie would go for. Living with Mrs. Canfield, huh? Are you as weird as her?" He clinched his fists, hoping for a fight. Maybe, if he proved he was the better man by beating this skinny bookworm, it would impress Laurie.

Dan turned white. He would love to knock some of the cockiness out of the big bull. But he had never been in a real fistfight in his whole life. He didn't have the slightest idea of how to defend himself. Not only was Bill far more experienced, he also outweighed him by a least seventy pounds.

Dan considered his options. Perched on the ladder with Bill standing in front, he couldn't just back away and leave. He would have to somehow talk himself out of it. "Look friend."

"I ain't your friend."

"Okay, okay. But why fight? It's obvious you have the winning edge. Besides, you look like you're all cleaned up to go somewhere. Why bother to get dirty in a fight you already know you'll win?"

Bill was taken by surprise. "You're admitting I'm the better man?"

Dan's face turned red with anger. In a controlled voice, he said, "I'll admit you can beat me when it comes to fist-fighting."

Bill looked at Laurie in triumph. She gave him a cold shoulder. His smiled faded.

A horn blasted, startling them all. An old pickup truck pulled over to the curve. The driver yelled, "Come on Bill! We're running late."

Bill waved to the driver, then turned and grinned maliciously at Dan. "Be seeing you." He gave Laurie a parting, wistful look and strolled to the truck.

Dan leaped off his ladder, embarrassed that Laurie had witnessed the whole thing. He jerked the ladder up and shifted to the next window. He must seem like a real sissy to her for not fighting, even when it was obvious he couldn't win. He rammed the ladder hard onto the ground, wishing it were Bill.

Laurie began to thaw. She smiled weakly at Dan. "You handled that well. But I should caution you about Bill. He's the neighborhood thug. He's been in and out of trouble with the law ever since his dad deserted his family when Bill was ten."

Dan didn't catch Laurie's compliment. Heading up the ladder, his mind was on Bill. "He has a real vicious streak in him."

Laurie blurted, "You don't know how vicious!"

His startled expression prompted her to explain. "Four years ago some of the neighborhood pets were tortured and killed. Everyone knew Bill was doing it, but no one could prove it." Laurie's dark eyes flooded. "I found my cat, Sally, hanging from the apple tree in our backyard. Her throat had been cut." Forcing back her tears, she added, "Her back paws and tail were nearly burned off."

"My God!" Dan's stomach churned. "That's sick."

She nodded. "When Margaret saw Sally she marched straight to Bill's house. I don't know what she said to him and his mother. But since that time, no one has bothered our pets."

"Margaret? You mean Mrs. Canfield?"

"That's right. Didn't she ask you to call her Margaret?"

"Yes, but I don't feel comfortable doing that. It's not businesslike."

"You'd better, if you want to please her. She says Mrs. Canfield is her formal name and should be used only in formal relationships. You can't live with someone and stay formal for long, can you?"

"You can try!" Embarrassed by the start his outburst gave Laurie, he continued in a more polite tone. "I would prefer my relationship with Mrs. Canfield stay as formal and distant as possible without causing trouble."

"Why?"

"She's too strange. That's all."

"Oh, I get it. She told you about her gift. Well, for your information, Margaret is one of the kindest and most generous persons you'll ever meet. Years ago my mother was in a bad auto accident. She was in and out of hospitals for over two years. Margaret helped take care of me the whole time because I was too little to go to school like my sister and brother. She not only has been like a second mother to me; she has also been there whenever I needed a confidant. She is the smartest person I know."

"She's just an old woman."

"So? What law says an old woman can't be wise?"

"But, she's crazy. She thinks she can communicate psychically with animals."

"She can."

"Nobody can talk with animals like that." Dan shook his scraper at her. "Name me just one other person, besides Mrs. Canfield, who claims they can communicate with animals."

"I'll name two. Beatrice Lydecker and J. Allen Boone."

"Who?"

"Beatrice Lydecker wrote *What the Animals Tell me*. J. Allen Boone wrote *The Language of Silence* and *Kinship With All Life*. There are also numerous other books about talking with animals. And some gifted people probably keep their ability a secret from fear of being ridiculed."

"That's all a bunch of nonsense. I don't care what you, those writers, or Mrs. Canfield says. It's not possible."

Laurie sighed. "Look. Let's don't risk ruining what could be the start of a good friendship. It's ridiculous to argue about something that time and circumstances will prove one way or another. Why don't we drop the subject?"

Dan was relieved. He didn't like being angry with someone as appealing as Laurie. "Agreed." He stretched his hand down to her. "Let's shake on it."

There was a mischievous, knowing gleam in Laurie's dark eyes as they shook hands. "These next three years could prove very interesting."

They heard a screen door opening. An older, plumper version of Laurie called from her front porch. "Laurie, I need your help in the kitchen."

Laurie waved at her. "Okay, Mom. I'm coming." She headed toward home, then suddenly spun around. Cupping her hand to her mouth, she yelled back. "It could be *very* interesting." She broke into an impish laugh that hung in the air after she had disappeared.

With her teasing words still ringing inside his head, Dan returned to his scraping. His mind whirled, recalling all those he had met and heard in the past twenty-four hours. Not watching what he was doing, he gouged the wood. He cursed, then mumbled under his breath, "Everyone in this neighborhood is nuts." He glanced at Laurie's house. "Even the cute ones are crazy."

Deciding it was best if he pushed the whole thing out of his mind, he tried to concentrate on the job at hand. However, for the rest of the day he worked with a fury that would have amazed his father.

CHAPTER TWO

The evening breeze ruffled the curtains in Dan's room. Too engrossed to notice, Dan sat hunched over his desk with his English textbook and class notes spread out before him. Two weeks into the summer session, he faced his first important test the next morning. He was worried. Professor Higgins had a reputation for giving hard exams. Dan's dark brooding eyebrows joined over his nose as he frowned at his notes. Learning to study had been more difficult than he had figured.

Taylor leaped onto his desk, startling him. "Go away!"

The old yellow cat rubbed against his arm, blocking his view of his notes. Throwing his pen down, Dan scowled at the cat. "Why can't you leave me alone?"

Taylor sat down on the textbook and calmly stared back. Since the day Dan arrived, the feline had continuously followed him throughout the house, paraded across his homework, batted at his pen when he tried to write, and made a general nuisance of himself. Dan had tried shoving him aside, ignoring him, and pleading with him. Once he shut him out of his room, but the cat made such a loud fuss that Dan had to let him back in.

The one thing Dan hadn't tried, short of killing, was to complain to Margaret. He was still leery of her and unsure of how she would react to one of her annoying cats being criticized. Who knew what someone as weird as she would do. "What am I going to do with you?" he asked the cat.

Taylor yawned.

Dan sighed. "Okay. Let's try again." He shoved the cat off the textbook and tried to return to his studying. Purring, Taylor rubbed against Dan and flipped his tail in his face.

"That does it." Dan grabbed the cat, dropped him in the hallway, and slammed the door shut.

Taylor clawed at the bottom of the door, attempting to pull it open. Pressing his hands over his ears, Dan tried to concentrate on his notes. The clawing intensified. Dan shoved a finger in each ear. Taylor cried pathetically. Dan hurled his dictionary at the door. "Go away!"

Blessed silence prevailed for a few minutes. Then the clawing started again. Dan yelled, "Leave me alone. I need to study."

Taylor bawled.

Defeated, Dan threw open the door. Taylor bounded for Dan's desk, where he settled down on the textbook and proceeded to clean himself. Dan stood by the door, too dejected to move.

Carrying freshly laundered linens, Margaret appeared at the top of the stairs. "What's wrong?"

Dan knew he was beaten. There was nothing left to do but take his chances and tell her. He pointed a shaking finger at the happy cat. "I can't study with him bothering me; but when I close him out of my room, he claws at the door and meows."

"I see." She smiled at Taylor as she thought for a minute, then turned to Dan. "Wait here. I'll be right back."

She returned with an old, white bath towel. Folding it, she laid the towel across a back corner of the desk. She shifted Taylor from book to towel. Gently holding his head, she looked into his face and said, "Now, Taylor, this is your spot. You can be with Dan as much as you like as long as you stay here and leave him alone while he's working." To Dan's amazement, Taylor sank contentedly down on the towel.

Margaret glanced at Dan. "This arrangement wouldn't work with Katy and Princess. They have different temperaments. But it will suit Taylor just fine."

Grateful, and surprised at Margaret's gracious understanding of his problem, he meekly said, "Thank you."

"You're welcome." She gave the yellow cat one last stroke. "I'll leave you two alone now."

Afraid some movement of his part would cause Taylor to get up, Dan slowly approached his desk and eased into the chair. Taylor stayed where he was. Relieved, Dan soon became engrossed again in his studies. He glanced up every time Taylor shifted positions, fearing the cat would bother him again, but Taylor always settled back down on the towel.

Late afternoon of the next day, Dan was gathering up his tools after having fixed a sagging gate that boarded the Carpenter's property. Laurie's ride pulled up to drop her off from her summer job. Dan was pleased to see her again. They hadn't had an opportunity to speak since their first meeting. Though he couldn't put his finger on why, there was something about her that he found intriguing.

She waved at him and strolled over. Pointing to Taylor watching from Margaret's window, she said, "I see you have an audience."

Dan frowned. "He always has to be where I am. At least he doesn't follow me outdoors."

"Old Taylor never was much for the outdoors. Several years ago, he lost a fight with a young tomcat. After that, he stopped going out entirely."

"Why is he always watching me?"

She shrugged. "Of all the cats Margaret has had, Taylor is the most psychic. Maybe he senses something about you that he finds fascinating."

The look in her dark eyes proclaimed that Taylor wasn't the only one who found him interesting. Dan blushed. Laurie smiled impishly. Dan's face reddened more. Laurie's dimples deepened. Dan squirmed and glanced around, trying to avoid eye contact.

His eyes lit on Taylor in the window, giving him his out. Feeling in control again, he faced Laurie. "Taylor kept me from studying yesterday until Margaret got him to stay put while I worked. If she'd really been able to communicate with animals the way she claims, she would've told Taylor to stay totally away from me."

"Not necessarily."

"Huh?"

"She may not want Taylor to leave you *completely* alone."

"Why not?"

"Why don't you ask her?"

Suspecting Laurie wouldn't approve of his resolve to keep communication with Margaret on a business-only level, he shrugged and said, "I wouldn't feel comfortable talking to her about it, that's all. You tell me."

"Okay. But you're not being fair to Margaret."

Dan couldn't help noticing how charming she looked with her round nose wrinkling as she thought. She smiled at him. "First, Margaret likes to see her animals happy. If Taylor wants to be with you, and there's no harm in it, why not satisfy him?"

Unable to come up with an answer, he motioned for her to continue. "Secondly, and I suspect most importantly, Margaret probably figures Taylor has something to teach you."

"Teach me!" What could a cat teach me?"

"All life forms have truths to teach, if you open yourself to the idea and learn how to pay attention. Didn't Job, in the Bible, urged his friends to let the earth, beasts, birds, and even fish teach them? Maybe Margaret figures Taylor can teach you to appreciate cats. It's true you don't like them, isn't it?"

"How did you know that?"

"Margaret told me."

"What!"

"Don't get all concerned. It doesn't worry her. She said the only reason you hate cats is because you've never been around them. That all you know is what you've heard—mostly myths and half-truths. And that you feel it's somehow unmanly to like them."

Annoyed that they had made him a topic of discussion and that Margaret had hit too close to the truth, he blurted, "How can she know that?"

She shrugged. "How does she know anything?"

Dan frowned at her. He wasn't about to start *that* argument again. Margaret was plain crazy. And that was that. Closing up his toolbox, he said, "Look, I've got to fix a loose hinge on the backdoor, then get cleaned up for supper."

"I understand. I've got to get busy myself." Curious to see his reaction, she explained, "I've got a date tonight."

Dan felt his heart give a lurch. Why hadn't it occurred to him that she might be dating? It would be natural for a girl as cute as she was to have lots of boyfriends. And why did he feel such a sudden pang of jealousy? It was none of his business who she dated. Yet he found himself asking, "Is it with a steady boyfriend?"

His question raised her hopes. "No, just a friend." To make sure he knew she was available, she added, "I don't have any serious relationships going at the moment."

Taken back by her obvious opening, he grabbed up his toolbox to leave. Besides not having either the time or money to date, he was realistic enough to know that a romantic entanglement would distract him too much from his studies and put his college career in jeopardy. Walking to classes and eating lunch together, as friends, should be safe enough. But anything resembling a date with anyone was out of the question. At least until he had succeeded in putting his academic probation solidly behind him.

Not knowing what else to say, he blurted out, "Have a good time on your date." Irritated with himself for caring if she did or didn't and for hoping she wouldn't, he stomped away.

Laurie turned toward her house, puzzled and hurt by his cool reaction, and fearful that she had blown her chances by being too forward.

Several weeks passed. It was a hot, humid July afternoon. Margaret's two-story home didn't have central air-conditioning. A window fan, aided by a large maple tree shading the corner of the house, kept Dan's bedroom bearable. He sat at his desk working on an assignment for Math 132. The sounds of the phone ringing downstairs and of Margaret picking it up distracted him. Throwing his pencil down, he slumped back in his chair. A math problem had him stumped, and the weather wasn't helping his concentration.

Noticing Dan had quit, Taylor rose from his towel and arched his back in a good stretch. He strolled over to Dan and rubbed his head against his hand. Dan frowned. While Taylor still left him alone when he studied, the old feline insisted on attention whenever he took a break. Giving in, Dan reluctantly scratched the purring cat's head with one hand, while picking up his ice tea glass with the other. He took a long, cooling drink and held the glass against his sweaty forehead.

"Dan," Margaret called from the foot of the stairs. "Can you quit for awhile?"

Dan glanced at his homework. "Yeah, sure," he yelled. "I could use a break." Taylor followed him downstairs.

Always classy looking, even in faded denim jeans and a light pink summer top, Margaret held her purse and car keys. "I'd like you to come with me. If things go as I hope, I might need your help."

Dan waited until she had turned her old, green Buick into the street before asking, "Where are we going?"

Margaret switched on the air-conditioning. "Did you know that Laurie has an older sister named Sharon?"

"I know she has a brother in the army and a sister who is an elementary teacher. But I don't recall hearing their names."

"The sister is Sharon, and she just phoned me. She and her husband, Tom Rivers, bred their AKC registered Labrador retriever several months ago. They have a half-grown female pup they can't sell. It's too timid. Tom wants to have her put to sleep. Sharon begged me to check the pup out. She hopes I can figure a way to save it."

There was a hint of excitement in Margaret's voice. "I didn't tell Sharon, but I think this is the dog I've been waiting for. I've been looking for one ever since Toby died last year."

Getting excited himself at the prospect of having an animal in the house that he could enjoy, he forgot his resolve not to get personal. "Why didn't you get one sooner. Good dogs are a dime a dozen."

Margaret shot him a look that would have stopped a mad wolf in its tracks. Dan slouched in his seat. Several uncomfortable minutes past while Margaret focused on her driving.

Finally, she said, "Most good dogs can get along fine with the average unenlightened family. Certain dogs, however, make desirable pets only if they are treated with more understanding than the average family possesses. I've been waiting for a dog needing someone like me."

"But very few people have your..." He had to swallow before getting out the word, "Gift." Aren't there people without your ability who can give those special dogs what they need?"

"Of course. Best-of-breed humans."

Dan straightened. "What?"

"Owners with championship qualities. A best-of-breed human is long-suffering and kind. He is neither arrogant toward his pets, nor easily provoked. He does not concern himself with just his needs, but also considers the emotional and physical needs of his pets. He possesses patience for teaching, love for developing oneness, and gentleness for gaining trust. Unfortunately, championship owners aren't as plentiful as the need for them."

Dan was taken aback. His mother had made him study the Bible enough for him to realize Margaret had applied Apostle Paul's description of Christian love and fruits of the spirit to her championship owners. It had never occurred to him that those same Christian qualities should be manifested toward animals. He didn't want to consider such an idea. He asked, "Isn't it insulting to categorize people as best-of-breed, or worse?"

"Perhaps." She turned into a new subdivision swarming with playing children. She slowed down. "Yet, why should it be anymore demeaning to apply it to people than it is to apply it to any of God's other creatures?"

"I never thought about it before." He threw up his hands. "I don't know."

Margaret chuckled. "Maybe you should think on it."

Dan said, "I will", while knowing he wouldn't.

Margaret pulled into the driveway of a modest ranch-style home. "You probably should know." She nodded toward the house. "Sharon's husband would be angry if he knew she had called me. Tom is fond of animals, but he harbors several misconceptions about them that he won't allow anybody to challenge. He thinks I'm either crazy or a con artist." Dan struggled to appear outwardly sympathetic while smiling inwardly. Tom sounded like someone he could finally relate to.

They stepped from the cool automobile into the sultry July heat. Sharon flung open the door before they reached the front stoop. Her central air-conditioning was like a welcome mat bidding them to enter. The light beige living room was modestly furnished. Dan and Margaret settled on a colonial-style sofa, while Sharon perched on the arm of a matching chair.

Sharon's hazel eyes darted from front door to picture window, like a child worried about getting caught doing something wrong. Dan couldn't help comparing her to Laurie. She was more petite than Laurie. Where Laurie's hair was ash brown, Sharon's was mousy blonde. Most of all, Sharon lacked Laurie's lively sparkle.

Her pale eyes settled on Margaret. "Thank you for agreeing to come while Tom is still at work. I didn't know what else to do. Tom plans to have the pup put to sleep this weekend. If I weren't so desperate, I would never risk upsetting him by calling you. We've tried everything to find a home for the pup. We even offered to give her away after we found we couldn't sell her. But no one wants a dog that won't stay in the same room with them."

"Don't worry," Margaret answered. "We'll figure something out before Tom gets home."

Sharon smiled trustingly at her and relaxed. "I knew I did right in calling you." She glanced curiously at Dan.

"Oh my," exclaimed Margaret. "Where are my manners. Sharon, this is Dan Hanley. He is boarding with me while attending the university."

"Oh course," Sharon said, scrutinizing him. "I should have guessed. Laurie has told me all about you. She is quite taken with you."

Dan recognized the matchmaker glint in Sharon's eyes. He shifted nervously. He wasn't going to become involved with Laurie, or anyone else. Getting his degree had to be his one and only interest, if he was going to make it. He decided a change of subject was needed. "So, you have a shy pup."

Her smile disappeared. "That's right. We've been calling her Sobra. It's a Spanish word. It means 'leftover'. We pronounce it without the Spanish accent."

She turned to Margaret. "We didn't know Sobra was timid until the pups were old enough to sell. She never acted shy around our friends who played with the litter. When buyers started coming, you couldn't tell her from any other pup as long as they were looking the whole litter over. But the second a buyer picked her out for a closer look, she ran. She would hide behind me, shivering. No amount of coaxing would get her to move. If I tried holding her so the buyer could check her out, she fought so hard I had to put her down to keep from dropping her.

"I started working with her separately, to see if I could help her get over her shyness. That's when we learned she's afraid of any strange noises or objects she hasn't encountered before. I don't understand it. She gets really frightened. Neither Tom nor I have ever mistreated her. We've never even struck her, or any of the pups. And her mother isn't timid, so she couldn't have gotten it from her."

Margaret thought for a minute. "I have the feeling that something occurred when she was very tiny. Probably before her eyes were opened. Can you recall anything unusual happening during those first ten days?"

"Well." She hesitated. "There is one thing I've wondered about. We made a temporary enclosure to keep the newborn pups off our cold concrete basement floor. We covered a slightly elevated plywood sheet with shredded newspapers. Tom put boards around it to form a pen, but he didn't do a good job of securing them.

"There were a few times when I heard a pup crying and checked on it. Somehow it had gotten separated from the rest and was trapped between the plywood and a board that kept working loose. Each time, I comforted the pup, put it back with the rest, and replaced the board. Since the majority of the pups were the same sex, color, and size, I was never sure if it was the same pup or a different one each time. The problem stopped when their eyes opened."

Margaret sat quietly for a minute with her eyes closed. "That's it. It was the same pup. Being separated and trapped when blind and helpless conditioned her to be afraid of anything unfamiliar. When a buyer signaled her out, the old fear at being separated took over. She hid behind you because you were the one who always rescued her before when she was trapped."

"Won't such early negative conditioning be impossible to overcome?"

"For a lot of people, yes. It would take more time, patience, work, and understanding than most are willing to give. But it's not hopeless. Sobra does have one thing going for her."

"What's that?"

"She's obviously intelligent. She knew the difference between buyers interested in separating her from the only security she's known and visitors who posed no such threat. I would like to see her now, please."

Sharon remained seated on the arm of her chair. "Before I get her," she said, looking embarrassed. "Could I ask another favor of you?"

"What is it?"

"Something has been bothering me ever since the litter was born. Lady went into labor the same evening we were scheduled to play cards at a friend's home. I tried to talk Tom into either canceling out or asking our friends to move the card party here, where we could keep an eye on Lady. I told Tom you had said some pregnant dogs want their owners nearby when they're in labor, and I felt Lady was one of them. But you know Tom. He said that was a bunch of nonsense. That dogs don't have emotional feelings or needs."

Margaret expelled a lady-like snort of contempt. She said, "Go on."

"All the pups had arrived by the time we returned home. "We found seven black, live pups—and one dead. It was a female and the largest of the litter. Tom said it was to be expected. That it was normal to lose one or two pups during birthing. But I can't shake the feeling we could have saved this one if we'd stayed home."

"I see. You want me to try to pick up what happened from Lady."

"If you wouldn't mind. I'd really appreciate it. It may give me some peace of mind."

"All right."

"Lady's in the backyard with the pup. I'll get her." She disappeared into the kitchen.

Feeling trapped, Dan glanced at Margaret. She had her eyes closed as if meditating. Dan frowned. The last thing he wanted was to see a demonstration of her so-called gift. A repressed worry floated to the surface of his mind. What if she proved she really did have psychic ability? Did that mean she was evil like the church he was raised in claimed? He wouldn't dare live with her if that were so. Yet, how could he get his degree in three years if he didn't? He was distracted by the sound of a dog running across the kitchen's vinyl flooring.

A black Labrador retriever, about two and a half years old, burst into the living room. With tail wagging at top speed, she sniffed the visitors over. She shifted back and forth between them, accepting their petting as her due. Her thick tail beat relentlessly against the coffee table.

Sharon sank down in her chair. Margaret waited for Lady to finish her greeting ritual and calm down; then she pushed the coffee table away and ordered Lady to lie at her feet. With quizzical expression, Lady obeyed.

Margaret shifted her body and pulled on her jeans in an effort to get more comfortable. She straightened her back, placed her feet flat on the floor, and rested her hands, palms up, on her lap. She closed her eyes and breathed deeply several times. Then she sat quietly, trying to calm her mind to a deep alpha level. She glanced at Lady, who stared back. Margaret mentally addressed the dog, then closed her eyes and waited for the impressions to emerge from the depths within her.

Muted voices of children playing outside in the street were the only sounds penetrating the stillness.

Margaret spoke in a soft monotone. "I'm getting images of the basement. There is a large cardboard box lying on its side, lined with shredded newspapers and sitting on raised plywood sheeting. The boards surrounding the box and plywood are low enough for Lady to step over, but high enough to keep newborn pups in." She hesitated, waiting for more to come to her.

Taking a deep breath, she continued. "Lady is in the cardboard box. She is continually shifting positions, and whining. She's hurting and she doesn't understand what's happening to her." With eyes closed, Margaret leaned toward Sharon. "This was her first litter, wasn't it?"

"Yes."

Margaret straightened and sat quietly for a moment before speaking. "Lady continues to whimper. She longs for the reassuring presence of her humans. The pains get closer together. She stops whining. An urge to push overwhelms her. She yelps in pain as the first pup, a large one, is born. The sharp, searing pain takes her by surprise. She focuses on her rear, licking and cleaning, trying to soothe the ache. She is not cognizant of the puppy, lying encased in an unbroken amniotic sac.

"Lady concentrates on her throbbing rear until her pains intensify again and she gets the urge to push. The second pup is smaller. Its birth isn't nearly as painful and its sac is broken. The smell of amniotic fluid triggers Lady's instincts. She sniffs the wet newborn, gives it an experimental lick, and then begins cleaning it up.

"After she's done, she glances around and, for the first time, notices her first-born pup. She breaks the amniotic sac and starts to clean the pup. She whimpers when it doesn't respond to her licking. She nudges it and licks harder. But it's no use. It's dead." Margaret leaned back, opened her eyes, and glanced around.

An unchecked tear rolled down Sharon's cheek. "I knew it. I just knew it. If we'd stayed home, I would've broken the sac so that helpless puppy could breathe. It died because we left an inexperienced dog alone."

Margaret pulled a tissue from her purse and shifted to the arm of Sharon's chair. Handing Sharon the tissue, she said, "I'm sorry. Maybe it would have been better if I hadn't told you."

"No." Sharon wiped her eyes. "I wanted to know. I had to know." She leaned against Margaret, who placed an arm around her and tried to comfort her.

Dan scowled at the two women. He didn't know with whom he felt the most contempt—Margaret, for making up such a story, or Sharon, for being gullible enough to believe it.

He had to give Margaret credit. She put on a good act. She knew enough about the birthing process of dogs and the layout of Sharon's basement to make it sound convincing. There wasn't one solid piece of evidence to prove that she'd received any information psychically. The whole thing was a fabrication. He knew she favored the neutering of animals to control kitten and puppy overpopulation problems. She probably figured if she put a big enough guilt trip on Sharon, Sharon would nag Tom into having Lady spayed.

Dan leaned back, relieved that he had discovered Margaret was only a shyster. He glanced at the guilt-saddened Sharon; all his contempt shifted to Margaret. If he weren't compelled to stay on her good side for the sake of room and board, he'd let her know he was onto her and march out of her life.

Sharon glanced at her watch and sprung upright in her chair, almost causing Margaret to lose her balance. "It's getting late. Tom will be home soon and you haven't even seen Sobra yet." She jumped up. "The rest of the litter has been sold for quite awhile. Tom says there's no reason for holding off putting the pup to sleep. He wants to get it over with."

Wanting to feel helpful, Dan asked, "Why don't you just keep her if she's happy with you?"

"I'd like to. I've grown attached to her. But Tom says our house is too small for two big dogs, and that the pup isn't good for anything. Not even for breeding. She would pass her timidness on to her pups."

Margaret chuckled. "At least Tom and I agree on one thing. She should never be bred." She glanced at Lady still lying by the sofa. "Sharon, take Lady out so she won't get in the way."

"Come on Lady." Not wanting to obey, Lady looked pleadingly at Margaret. Sharon grabbed her collar. "Come on." Reluctantly, Lady rose to her feet and followed Sharon into the kitchen. Margaret shifted back to her original place on the sofa, beside Dan.

The sounds of a struggle came from the kitchen. Sharon yelled from the back door, "Lady never wants to leave when there's company, and the pup senses someone is here. She's afraid to come in." Sharon hassled with the dogs a couple of more minutes. Then came a frustrated command. "Out!" They heard the door slam shut, and Sharon's relieved voice. "Finally."

There was the sound of toenails scraping the floor. Petite Sharon came into view, dragging a half-grown Labrador by a collar made from a man's belt. The black pup was doing her best to dig in with all four paws, but she couldn't get traction on the kitchen's vinyl floor.

Sharon pulled her to the doorway where the frightened pup caught sight of Margaret and Dan. The dog burst into a silent frenzy, violently jerking her head and trying to break Sharon's grip. Sharon held on with both hands. "She usually acts this way only when we're trying to show her to a potential owner. I thought she would be calmer with you."

While Sharon tried to keep the dog from dragging her back into the kitchen, Margaret looked around the living room. "Her fear is too intense, we need to get her calmed down before I can communicate with her." She pointed to a green recliner in the corner nearest Sharon. "Dan, you move that chair to one side. Sharon, take Sobra to the corner and squat in front of her. Use your body to block her view as best you can."

Dan shifted the recliner as Sharon pulled the jerking pup into the room. The half-grown Lab gained a better toehold in the carpeting. Sharon's face reddened as she yanked the balking dog forwards an inch at a time. Getting out of the way, Dan moved back to the sofa. He was amazed that the dog neither growled nor attempted to bite Sharon. Sharon finally forced Sobra into the corner and squatted in front of her. "Sit." The pup sat, and shivered. She gave every indication that she would bolt any second. Both dog and woman were breathing heavily.

"Good," Margaret said. "Now I want us all to sit quietly for a minute and project reassuring, loving thoughts to Sobra. Sharon, you comfort her by touch as well. Lightly scratch her either on the rump just above her tail or on the chest between her front legs, whichever she likes best."

Dan and Sharon obeyed. Dan only partially. He sat quietly, but wasn't about to send any thoughts. The idea of projecting thoughts to anyone, let alone a dog, was pure nonsense. Besides, it wasn't manly.

Both the dog's and Sharon's breathing began to return to normal. The nervous pup peeked around Sharon at Margaret and Dan. There was a questioning look in her brown eyes every time they lit on Margaret. The minutes crawled by. Dan started to feel bored. The only sounds were the muted voices of the neighborhood children still playing outside and the low hum of the air-conditioner.

In a soft voice, Margaret said, "Sharon, I'm going to ease slowly toward you. Dan, don't make any sudden moves. We don't want to frighten her again." She crawled slowly to the corner.

The pup shifted. Sharon stroked her. "You're fine. There's nothing to be afraid of. She's not planning to take you away." The dog made a move to leave. Sharon tightened her grip on the makeshift collar. "You're fine."

Margaret eased into a sitting position behind Sharon. "Sharon, I am going to reach around you and join you in petting the pup. When I say 'now' I want you to crawl over me and sit by Dan. Remember no quick movements."

The pup slowly began to relax. Margaret whispered, "Now."

Sobra whined as Sharon crept away. Margaret tried to distract the dog by saying, "What a good pup you are." The troubled dog's eyes shifted back and forth between the two women, as if her sense of loyalty was being torn. Margaret stroked her gently, and spoke to her as if she were an equal. "You are a beautiful dog. You have a nice, healthy coat and an alert, intelligent face." The pup started to wag her tail. She halted and watched Sharon sit down on the sofa.

Margaret said, "What a good dog." The pup's attention shifted to Margaret. Cautiously, she sniffed the air in front of Margaret's face. The woman sat still and, as the dog gained courage, allowed the pup to give her a thorough going over. Sobra sighed and sank down with her front paws and head across Margaret's lap. Several minutes passed in silence while Dan and Sharon watched Margaret make over the dog. They all jumped when the front door opened.

A stocky-built, redheaded young man closed the door behind him. He wore a gray auto mechanic's uniform. "What's going on here?"

"Tom." Sharon leaped up. She glanced at her watch. "I let the time get away from us." She pointed to Dan, who stood up. "This is Dan Hanley, Margaret's boarder." She added apologetically, "I haven't started supper yet."

Tom nodded curtly at Dan. "Sharon, you know what I told you. Why is Margaret here?"

Margaret spoke up. "I came to buy a dog."

"What?"

She glanced from Tom to a surprised Sharon, then to Sobra resting with her head on her lap. She smiled at the pup. "I want this dog. I'm prepared to pay full price for her." Hesitantly, the pup wagged its tail.

Tom said, "But the trainer I consulted said she was too timid and high strung. She should be destroyed."

"Nonsense. Sometimes a timid animal that hasn't been handled right will have to be destroyed. Most will make fine pets if they get owners who know how to properly deal with their fears. That's all this pup needs. You want my money, or not?"

"Sure." He shrugged. "Why not? As long as you understand we won't take her back or refund your money if she's not satisfactory."

"Agreed. You fill out her papers and I'll write the check. Dan, hand me my purse." When they finished the paperwork, Margaret and the dog rose together. "Since she is use to it, I think I'll continue to call her Sobra."

After Margaret finally managed to coax the panicky pup into the back seat of her Buick, she handed Dan her car keys. "You drive. I want to sit in the back with Sobra."

"Okay. You're the boss."

Sobra was beginning to trust the woman; but, in spite of Margaret's reassurance, she did not trust either the strange moving contraption she was trapped in or the brooding man in front. Afraid to look out, she sank down on the seat and shivered in fright the whole way home. She vomited on the back seat just as Dan turned into the alley.

CHAPTER THREE

The leaves were turning to hues of orange, yellow, red, and brown. A few drop-offs floated gently to earth. The fall term was in full swing, and Laurie had joined Dan on his track back and forth to the university. On a bright Friday afternoon, they met in front of the student center to head home. The day had grown Indian summer warm. Dan held Laurie's books while she removed her jacket and draped it over her arm. She smiled a thank you.

Dan swallowed. Would he ever get use to those sexy dimples? His heart bounced like a basketball every time she looked at him that way, as if she wanted to kiss him. Resisting the urge to pull her to him, he hurriedly turned away from her and headed down the crowded sidewalk.

Laurie ran to catch up with him. Worried she had somehow annoyed him, she tried to change his mood. "I've been aiming to ask you. What do you think of Sobra now that you've lived with her for a few months?"

Dan smiled. "She's a wonder. I'll have to give Margaret credit for one thing. She knows her dogs. I wouldn't have given you one penny for that dog when I first saw her. After we got her home, Margaret let her explore all the rooms. She seemed to settle down then and appeared as calm as any normal dog.

"Then I flipped on the television set to catch the news. Sobra took a nosedive under an end table and crawled behind the sofa. Margaret coaxed her out, sat on the floor with her, and gradually got her to sniff the TV all over, so she would realize it was nothing to be afraid of.

"A couple of days later, Sobra was standing in the upstairs hallway, watching Margaret clean the bathroom. Margaret flushed the toilet. Sobra bolted down the stairs and slithered under the end table and behind the sofa so fast she knocked a lamp over, scaring herself even more. After that Margaret placed boards in front of the end tables' legs so Sobra couldn't get behind the sofa. She said she had to face her fears, not hide from them."

"Poor Sobra. It takes a lot of courage to face fears, for man or beast." As if quoting someone, she said, "Animals have a receptive mind when it comes to their owners' moods. If her fears had been merely the results of unconscious messages from Tom and Sharon, then changing to an owner with a different mindset would have automatically cured her. But Sobra's fears have been deeply ingrained by trauma-induced negative conditioning. That makes it a lot tougher for Margaret to overcome."

Dan didn't care for her authority sounding tone. "I suppose," he said nonchalantly.

They halted when they reached a busy street corner. Waiting with the crowd of college students for the light to change, Dan continued. "You should have seen Sobra when Margaret urged her to investigate the toilet. That big pup tiptoed towards it, all ready to run if that toilet dared make one false move. She tried to sniff it by stretching her nose as close as possible to it while keeping the rest of her as far away as possible." He chuckled. "Now we have to remember to keep the lid down because she wants to drink out of it."

Laurie laughed. Dan eyed her suspiciously. Surely, Margaret has kept her and her family well informed about Sobra's progress. Was Laurie trying to lead up to something?

The walk light changed. They turned down a side street, leaving the harried, crowded main thoroughfare behind. The peaceful, old residential area stretched before them, silently influencing them to slow down. A soft breeze rustled the trees. Falling leaves reminded them to take time to relish one of the few remaining, warm pleasant days.

Laurie took a deep breath, enjoying the autumn air. "Is Sobra doing better now?"

"She's improving every day. But has a long ways to go yet. Margaret keeps gradually introducing her to new things so she'll overcome her fears. When it's convenient, Margaret takes her along on car rides. At first Sobra had to be coaxed into the car. Now she races to the car and circles it until someone opens the door. Then she hops right in. One thing though, she won't sit up and look around when the car is moving. She lays on the back seat with her head down. I don't see how she can enjoy riding that way."

"She is probably just happy going with Margaret."

"I suppose."

Laurie gave him a searching, sideways glance. As she had hoped, talking about Sobra had put him in a more congenial mood. Now, she decided, was as good a time as any, to see if she could influence him. "Speaking of Margaret, have you formed any conclusions about her gift?"

He knew it. She *had* been leading up to something. He sighed in resignation. Now that she's brought it up, he might as well get it over with. "I'll agree Margaret is good with animals, but I can't see where her methods are any different from those of other good trainers. If she really did have the powers she claims, she would have used them to rid Sobra of her fears once and for all."

"You've been watching too many B movies."

"Huh?"

"Margaret has a gift, an ability. She doesn't possess unlimited powers. She is capable of communicating mentally with animals. She can sense their thoughts and feelings. And she can send them a sense of reassurance, trust, and love. She also sends them mental images of what she wants them to do or understand. But she doesn't have total power over their minds. No more than a teacher has full control over the minds of the students in her classroom.

"A teacher can be a strong, supportive, and important influence. But, ultimately, real learning only takes place when the students themselves open their minds and hearts—even if it's just a reluctant crack—to receive and ponder the lessons. It's the same with Margaret and Sobra."

"I suppose Margaret told you that?"

"That's right."

"I thought so. It makes a convenient excuse while handling Sobra like any other good trainer." He shifted his books and lifted his freed hand. His fingers made quotation marks in the air. "If her 'psychic message' doesn't work out the way it was expected then she can always fall back on blaming the animal."

Laurie lifted an eyebrow. "You still don't believe she can communicate psychically with animals, do you?"

"No."

"What about Lady's dead pup? Sharon told me you were there when Margaret found out what happened."

"It wouldn't be hard for someone with Margaret's knowledge of animals to fake the whole thing. She can sound very convincing."

Laurie stopped dead and stared at him in disbelief. She said angrily, "Margaret isn't the kind of person to do something like that. She would never lie. Especially when she knew it would upset Sharon. If you'd melt that icy wall you've built between you and her, you would realize that." With dark eyes flashing and back straight, she charged ahead. Dan decided it was best to remain discreetly silent while keeping up with her pace.

A block and a half later, she remembered why she had brought Margaret up in the first place and slowed down. You won't get anywhere by flaring up, she reminded herself. She calmly asked, "Why can't you be at least open to the possibility that such psychic abilities exist?"

He knew better than to get her dander up further by pointing out that, if such abilities did exist, they would have to be evil. Instead he said, "It's just not possible, that's all."

She snapped her fingers. "I get it. I know why you're so bull-headed." She spun around to face him. "You're a stuck adult."

"What?"

As if quoting again, she said, "Children are willing to explore new situations and ideas, and are continually open to learning and exploring more. People become stuck adults when they create an unquestioned, but firmly held, set of beliefs about how life is or should be. Then they close themselves off to learning from any situation that has the potential of challenging their convictions. Just like you, they are comfortable with the way they perceive the world and want nothing to do with anyone or anything that might cause them to start questioning the cherished beliefs they have based their whole lives and decisions on."

"What's so wrong with that?"

Laurie shrugged. "Maybe nothing. Only, didn't Jesus say we had to become like little children to inherit the kingdom of God?" She started walking again.

Dan eyed her uneasily. A part of him was sounding an alarm bell to change the subject quickly, before she got into areas he didn't want to deal with. But another part was curious. "How can you be like a child and still be a mature, responsible adult?"

Encouraged by his question, she said, "By viewing the world as one giant classroom. By realizing life is made up of a series of lessons—sometimes seemingly contradictory ones. By seeing every situation you are in as an opportunity for growth; your family provides the setting for one set of lessons, your job another, your hobbies and volunteer work still others. Some lessons overlap. And don't forget, nature also has important lessons to teach—perhaps the most important of all."

His expression communicated his disbelief. She let out a frustrated sigh. "Can't you see that you have been thrown in with Margaret for a reason? If you would open yourself up to exploring and learning from your situation, maybe you would quit being such a bull-headed, stuck adult."

"Huh! If you're so smart, what is the purpose behind all these so-called lessons we are all suppose to be learning?"

She shrugged. "To get us to know ourselves so we can recognize and eliminate those fears, attitudes, and beliefs that keep us from fully experiencing the kingdom of God within. To help you grow a little at a time toward full awareness of your oneness with God, or if you prefer, Universal Mind. Hindus and Buddhists refer to it as obtaining Nirvana."

Dan began to glance around nervously. Laurie was too carried away with her own rhetoric to notice. She continued, "In Christian terms, it means finding the kingdom of heaven within and manifesting the Christ, or Holy Spirit. Remember Jesus said he and God were one. He also declared what he could do, we could do. We need to be continually open to learning and growing toward oneness till the day we die—and beyond."

Dan was taken aback. He'd never heard such ideas expressed before. They sounded heretical, even dangerous. Jesus was the Son of God. Man wasn't capable of developing the same kind of oneness with God that he had. The alarm bell in his head was getting louder, warning him to have nothing more to do with Laurie. She was parroting someone who had brainwashed her. And her words sounded too much like that New Age thinking his mother had cautioned him about.

He fell silent, trying to decide what to do. It would be a lot easier if he didn't find her so appealing. He could sense her warmth, even now, while he was trying his best not to look at her.

Laurie studied his solemn face. "What's wrong? Did I hurt your feelings when I called you bullheaded?"

"No," he answered truthfully. "My parents have called me that for as long as I can remember. I'm use to it." He waited until they crossed a residential street before explaining. "I just don't like some of your ideas. That's all."

"Like what?"

He picked what he considered the safest area. Hesitantly, he said, "I still don't see what's so wrong with being what you call a stuck adult."

Sensing for the first time the level of his anxiety, Laurie considered dropping the whole thing. But she had been waiting a long time for this opening. Only she was aware of how deeply concerned Margaret was over Dan's coldness toward her. Wanting to help, Laurie was determined to take full advantage of this opportunity to try to influence him into changing his thinking.

Taking a deep breath, she said, "Besides stunting your own emotional and spiritual growth, being a stuck adult helps create a climate for conflict with others. Stuck adults feel they must protect themselves from those that have belief structures different from their own. Isn't that what you're doing with Margaret?"

Ignoring her question, Dan shrugged. "Everyone has to take a stand for what they believe in sometimes."

"True. But it's the methods that some use to protect themselves that's the problem. Eliminating the sources of conflicting ideas is one method. Elimination can range from mild censorship to wholesale slaughter of those who are different. Then there is denial. No matter how much evidence exists to support a conflicting viewpoint, a stuck adult denies it by either refusing to look at the proof or, when forced to confront it, to seriously consider it. Some will even try to destroy it."

She hesitated for a second at the sight of his stern face, thought of Margaret, then gathered up her courage to continue. "Another method is to label the person or idea with some name that makes the adult feel justified for not considering the viewpoint they represent. A lot of religious groups, Christian and non-Christian, are very adept at labeling all differing beliefs as evil."

She hit too close to home. He glared suspiciously at her. "How did you develop such crazy ideas?"

"Some from reading and thinking." She smiled sheepishly. "And the rest from Margaret."

"Margaret! I knew it. You have her on such a high pedestal you can't see that she has bamboozled you. She's nothing but a conniving old woman."

"I see. You think declaring that she is conniving releases you of any need to consider the possibility that her gifts might be real."

"That's right." He stared at her, confused by her smile. "What is so funny?"

"You just used the dismiss-it-by-labeling method."

Dan felt his face begin to burn. "Look. There is absolutely no proof that Margaret, or anyone else, can communicate psychically with animals. And that is that."

She chuckled, deepening her dimples. "You're using denial."

He shook his finger in her face. "For half-a-cent, I'd move out and leave you and Margaret to your weird ideas."

"Now you're threatening a form of elimination by removing yourself from the situation."

Dan stammered and shook his finger at her, unable to reply. Her grin faded. "I'm sorry, Dan. I didn't mean to get you so upset. Let's forget the whole thing. It's not worth hurting our friendship over. Is it?"

He dropped his hand. She looked as if she wanted to give him a kiss or hug, but was afraid to offer it. His anger cooled. He said, "No. It's not." But he wasn't so sure. Her willingness to believe everything

Margaret had told her meant she was gullible and untrustworthy.

In an obvious attempt to make amends, she said, "Let's change the subject completely. The theatrical department is sponsoring a series of classical movies. They're free for students with current ID. Tomorrow night's is *Rear Window* with Jimmy Stewart. I've always wanted to see it without TV commercials. Would you like to go with me?"

Dan glanced into her inviting, dark eyes, and repressed an urge to stroke her ash brown hair. He was sorely tempted to go. But he was still resolved not to risk any romantic involvement until he was well off probation. Her invitation was too close to being a date, at least the kind he could afford. Still, maybe just this one time wouldn't hurt. It was certain the walk home in the dark would lead to the kiss he ached to give her.

She smiled, deepening her sexy dimples. "If it's Margaret you're thinking about, don't worry. I'm sure she wouldn't mind setting aside any project she has for you long enough for you to go."

The mention of Margaret brought him up short. The entire conversation they had just had flashed through his mind. He thought of how his mother would react to her ideas. He eyed Laurie. He liked her a lot, maybe too much. With her mind so obviously contaminated by Margaret's beliefs, getting more involved with her could make his vow not to let anything change him harder to keep. No. It's better that they keep things the way they were.

"Thanks for asking, but I'm going to be busy this weekend helping Margaret clean out the basement, and working on a class report due Tuesday. I don't think I'd better take the time off."

Laurie's smile faded. "Oh. I understand."

Feeling guilty for disappointing her, he added, "I hope you won't miss the movie because of me."

"Don't worry. I won't. I'll call Stan Weatherby from my English class. He had already asked me, but I told him I'd have to let him know because I thought I might be already going with someone. He seems to be a real nice guy."

Dan was irritated with himself for feeling a pang of jealousy. "Good," he lied, "That makes me feel better."

They finished their walk in silence. The sound of a dog's frantic barking roused them. Alarmed, Dan said, "That's Sobra." They raced around the corner of Margaret's house, and halted at the side gate.

Outside of the gate to the alley, Bill Saxon was picking something up. Straightening, he hurled a small stone at Sobra. Luckily, the barking dog had backed close to the house, and Bill's aim was off. The stone landed in front of Sobra, joining several others he had pitched.

The hair of Sobra's back stood straight up. Nearly fully grown now, she barked with impressive, but deceptive, fury. She glanced at the doghouse by the backdoor, trying to decide to rather continue barking or run and hide. Dan knew that if even one of Bill's stones had hit her, she would be shivering in the doghouse. Bill primed for another throw.

"Hey!" Dan yelled across the yard. "Stop that!"

Bill tossed the stone up and down in his hand as he hollered back. "You'd better keep that dog from barking at me every time I walk down this alley."

"How can she be a good watch dog if she doesn't bark when someone comes near her property?"

"Who cares? I don't want no dumb dog barking at me. I'm warning you, you'd better make her shut up." He marched off down the alley, tossing the stone up and down in his hand.

Dan and Laurie entered the yard. With tail wagging, Sobra ran to Dan who dropped to one knee. The big black Lab squirmed with delight as Dan made over her.

Laurie nodded toward Bill disappearing around the corner. "Talk about ego. Bill takes it personally every time a dog barks at him. It would be funny if he didn't have such a vicious streak. Who knows what he might do." She glanced at the locked-up house. "By the way, where is Margaret?"

Dan scratched Sobra in a favorite spot behind her ear. "She said she'd been invited to give a lecture this afternoon to some women's group about the work of the shelter for homeless animals. I guess she's not back yet."

"It figures. Margaret does a lot of work for that shelter. They're one of the few groups in the country that don't put unwanted animals to sleep. They work hard trying to find good homes for needy animals, taking in the few they can, and supporting neutering programs. Since they get no public support and are totally dependent on private donations, Margaret is always willing to speak to anyone who might give them some help."

Dan had heard enough about Margaret and her ideas for one day. He gave Sobra a final pat on the head and picked up his books. "Look, I have to fix a loose railing on the front porch before I can get started on my homework. See you Monday morning as usual?"

"Okay." She started to leave, then spun around. "You'd better warn Margaret about Bill."

"I will." He watched Laurie until she had disappeared into her house. He sighed. In spite of her misguided beliefs about Margaret, she was still the most exciting girl he'd ever met. With Sobra beside him he headed towards the backdoor, wishing things were different.

Later that evening, a stretched out Sobra slept beside Margaret's kitchen chair. Taylor and the gray cats, Katy and Princess, were curled up asleep on the throw rugs. Dan finished the last of his peach cobbler, then leaned back in his chair.

He took a sip of fresh-brewed coffee. "Laurie and I caught Bill Saxon throwing rocks at Sobra today. He warned me to stop her from barking at him."

Margaret grimaced and put her cup down. "Bill must have been up to something. He and his friends have been suspected in several recent house break-ins. I have tried to teach Sobra to bark only when someone is actually on or very close to my property, and not just passing by. With Bill and his friends roaming the neighborhood, I want to know when someone is around. Besides, Sobra derives a great deal of satisfaction from feeling she's helping me by barking a warning. I hate to deprive her of that pleasure."

She smiled at the sleeping dog. "It might be different if she were a real menace. Timid dogs either bite or run when feeling threatened. Sobra's no biter. Yet, she has a bark strong enough to bluff anyone who doesn't know her."

Dan leaned forward. "What about Bill?"

"Even if Bill could be trusted not to physically harm her, his teasing could prove damaging psychologically to a dog like Sobra. More than one dog has been ruined because of teasing or tormenting by ignorant children and adults.

"Just today, I met a lady, named Jan, at my lecture who told me about a small mixed breed she once owned. She said Macky always loved people and never caused a single problem. Then one summer evening Jan was sitting on her front porch with the dog besides her. Two teen-age boys walked past the house. With no warning, Macky bolted off the porch and attacked the bigger boy. The little dog hung onto the boy's leg with a fury Jan didn't know was in him. It took fifteen stitches to close the boy's wounds. His parents sued. The case was settled out of court.

"What disturbed Jan the most was Macky's uncharacteristic behavior. She thought she knew him. A neighbor woman enlightened her. When Jan went to work, she'd put Macky in a comfortable pen in her side yard. On several occasions, the neighbor saw the boy that Macky attacked torment the small dog. He'd poke at Macky with a stick until the dog was in frenzy. Luckily, there was an easy solution. The husband of

Jan's neighbor shifted Macky's pen to the backyard, out of sight of the street and temptation. Though Macky lived another three years, and continued to bare his teeth at teen-age boys, there were no more incidents.

"If teasing could make an even-tempered dog like Macky hyped up enough to attack, I'd hate to think what it would do to a timid one like Sobra."

Dan had grown fond of Sobra and wanted to help her. Besides he was feeling guilty for not acting more of a man to protect her. After thinking it over, he had decided a real man would have been able to take Bill on and teach him a lesson about throwing stones at confined dogs. He ignored the quiet voice at the back of his mind that said there was no way he could have done that and won.

He put his coffee cup down. "What can we do to protect Sobra?"

"I don't know. Give me a minute to think." She poured Dan a second cup of coffee and refreshed her own while he waited. "Even if I taught Sobra not to bark, it may not help her. Two of the dogs Bill tortured and killed a few years ago never barked at anyone. They were very friendly. But it didn't save them."

"While we are on the subject of Bill torturing animals. Laurie told me you stopped those neighborhood pet killings. What did you say to Bill?"

Margaret chuckled. "There are advantages to having ignorant people believe you're either crazy or evil. I told Bill that if he didn't stop bothering our pets, I'd put a curse on him. He was gullible enough to believe it." Her smile faded. "I've been afraid he might smarten up one day. His throwing those rocks at

Sobra today may be an indication he is losing his fear. If he is, we are going to have problems again. Unless something happens to send him to prison first."

Ignoring her reference to ignorant people, Dan said, "Maybe we should leave Sobra inside the house when we are both gone. It will give added protection to the house. Bill and his friends are less apt to break in with a large dog barking at them from inside."

"Good idea. We can let her out for exercise when we are around to hear her bark."

"There is one thing in her favor when she is outside."

"What's that?"

"If someone frightens her enough, she will run and hide in the doghouse. No one is likely to come into the yard and stick their hand in a doghouse with a dog her size in it."

"I hope you're right."

Dan helped Margaret clear the kitchen table. She handed him an empty plate. "You know, there is one other thing about Sobra that is beginning to worry me."

Dan placed the plate in the dishwasher. "What's that?"

"I know I'm in good health, but I have been sensing recently that I don't have more than two or three years left. I'm leaving most of my estate to the shelter for homeless animals with the understanding they will take care of any pets I leave behind.

"They will be able to handle the cats and bird all right, but Sobra could be another matter. The longer I work with her, the more trusting she's going to become. However, some of her old insecurities are bound to resurface at my death. If she's given to the wrong person, all my work could be undone."

"I wouldn't worry. You should have lots of years left. You'll probably outlive her."

"You could be right. If so, I wish I could shake the feeling that I don't. But to be honest with you. Except for what will happen to Sobra, it wouldn't bother me to cross over to the other side. Most of my friends and family, as well as my husband, are already there. This side is getting lonelier all the time. And the responsibilities I used to either enjoy or not mind are getting heavier and heavier to take care of."

She flipped off the kitchen light and went into the hallway to talk to Petey, her parakeet. Passing her, Dan headed up the stairway to start his homework.

He halted at the top of the stairs, startled because he suddenly realized he had just finished the most congenial and personal conversation he'd had with Margaret since he moved in. Their mutual concern for Sobra had caused him to forget his resolve to maintain a business-only distance.

Taylor rubbed against Dan's legs. Deep in thought, Dan unconsciously picked up the purring cat and rubbed his chin against Taylor's fur. He shook his head. On the surface Margaret appeared to be a fine lady. But in the future, he'd better be more careful about staying on his guard. It wouldn't do to become too friendly. Below the surface, she was still a shyster. And now, thanks to his conversation with Laurie, he knew she definitely wasn't a Christian according to the standards he had been taught.

CHAPTER FOUR

New record lows were set the January of Dan's first winter in college. It was bitter cold, with little snow. Dan and Laurie were too bundled up, shivery, and hurried to get out of the biting wind for more than the briefest of conversations on their trips back and forth to campus.

At Margaret's, Dan divided his time between schoolwork and building replacement storage cabinets for the basement. Margaret kept busy helping the shelter rescue animals exposed to the climate and counseling people on the proper care of their pets in minus zero weather.

The temperature warmed to the high 20's the first week of February. Then—as if winter had been saving the snow for one big dumping—the worse snowstorm in years struck. Two feet fell in a few short hours, followed by three days of lighter snow. Traffic snarled and halted. Businesses shut down, and rural schools closed for ten straight days. While Kyle University did not officially close, several of Dan and Laurie's classes were canceled because their professors could not get in from the country.

Dan welcomed the extra time to work on his basement wall cabinets' project. Making the three long cabinets had taken longer than he estimated. One Saturday, he was removing the last of the old storage cabinets when Margaret appeared at his side. She helped him jockey the first of the new cabinets into place and steadied it while he anchored it securely to the basement wall. They stepped back to look. Dan had selected high-grade plywood so he could finish them with the natural oak look Margaret wanted.

Margaret looked at the mounted cabinet and examined the two cabinets waiting to be hung. "They look good, Dan. Very professional. Now I can store my supplies without worrying that the shelves are going to collapse. Thank you."

Dan eyed his handiwork. Glowing from the satisfaction of a job well done, he said, "You're welcome." He glanced at Margaret. She appeared hesitant, as if wanting to say something. He asked, "What's the matter? Is there something about the cabinets you don't like?"

"No. The cabinets are fine. I was just wondering if I should ask a favor of you."

"What is it?"

"I know you've never said anything to me," she replied hesitantly. "But I sensed you were extremely uncomfortable when I demonstrated my gift with Lady on the day we got Sobra."

Not knowing how to reply, Dan kept silent.

"Don't worry. I am not going to hold it against you, and I'm not going to pressure you about it." Her gray-green eyes revealed a hidden pain, as she said, "I did that a long time ago with someone else and have paid a miserable price for my mistake ever since."

Dan was relieved, but curious, wondering if the price she paid had anything to do with her only son in California that she never hears from. He resisted the urge to ask; it wouldn't be business-like. Instead he asked, "Why are you bringing this up now?"

"After sensing how you felt, I decided never to ask you to accompany me on a consultation. But something has come up, and I need your help. I've received a phone call. A young couple has an unmanageable cat. They asked the shelter for homeless animals to take it; but, thanks to the bad weather, the shelter is already overcrowded with animals they have rescued. Rather than have the cat taken to the county animal shelter—where the odds are extremely good that it will be destroyed in three days or less—the homeless shelter urged the couple to contact me before giving up on it."

"What does that have to do with me?"

"The Davidsons live in a mobile home park ten miles out in the country. The rural roads are passable right now, and the wind is calm. The weatherman on this morning's news show predicted that it wouldn't pick up again until this evening. However, the north-south roads have only one lane open and are in danger of blowing shut if the wind would happen to pick up sooner than expected."

"I see," Dan said weakly. "You want me along in case you run into an unexpected problem."

"I would really appreciate it. I am getting too old to risk being stuck in a snow drift."

Dan wasn't at all anxious to watch Margaret fool the Davidsons the way she had Sharon. He rubbed his chin while trying to figure a way out of going. "Why can't they wait until next week. The roads should be clear by then."

"They adopted a toddler recently. They're afraid the cat will hurt her if they wait any longer."

"Why don't they bring the cat here?"

"It's better if I see the animal in its own environment."

Of course, Dan thought. Margaret would be able to pick up clues to make her act more convincing if she went to their home. He continued to stand, rubbing his chin, trying to think of an acceptable way out of going. Finally, he reluctantly said, "Okay. I'll go with you."

Margaret drove through the snow-entombed countryside without trouble. She pulled into a newly cleared space facing the side of a fairly new, white mobile home. Snow had drifted halfway up the side of the home. Someone had shoveled a path to clear the way to the landing and front door. They rang the doorbell, and a man, about thirty, let them in. Todd Davidson took their coats and offered them a seat on the brown sofa. They had to remove several toys before they could sit down.

A woman, also about thirty, entered through the kitchen area, carrying a squirming little girl about two years old. She shifted the child to her hip and held out her hand. "Hello my name is Katherine-- Kate for short." They shook hands.

Todd pointed proudly at the pretty blonde tot, struggling to be put down. "This is our Amy."

Kate shifted the child to her other arm. "Amy's natural mother was my sister. She was killed in an automobile accident not too long ago." Kate kissed the wiggling tot. "My sister and Amy's father weren't married. He denied being the father and left the state before Amy was born. We can't have children and wanted Amy, so the court granted us custody."

Kate gave up trying to hold the toddler and put her down. "We've had Cherish, our cat, for seven years. She was never any trouble until Amy came. We think she is jealous of the baby."

Amy headed for Margaret's purse, on the coffee table. Ignoring her, Kate continued. "We don't want to get rid of Cherish, but she's gotten so temperamental we can't trust her. She won't use her litter box, and she claws the drapes and furniture in Amy's room. Worst of all, she's scratched four people, including Amy."

She smiled at the little girl. "We can't have that."

Margaret reached for her purse as Amy grabbed the strap. Neither parent moved to restrain the child. Margaret smiled at the toddler tugging on her strap. "I'm sorry, Amy. My purse is not child proof. I wouldn't want it or you to come to any harm." She gently pried Amy's fingers from the strap and placed the purse on the back of the sofa.

Amy stared at Margaret in bewilderment, as if she had never been told "no" before. She puckered her face, stretched her hand toward the purse, and wailed.

Todd glanced at his watch. "Kate, why don't you put Amy to bed. It's close enough to her naptime. I'll go find Cherish." Kate carried the still demanding little girl out.

Todd returned with the cat. Placing her on the coffee table, he squatted down and held her there, stroking her. "Cherish's mother was a black mixed breed, and her father was a purebred Siamese. She inherited her mother's coloring and her father's body shape and temperament."

Dan studied her. A black Siamese was the best description anyone could ever give Cherish. Her yellow eyes fascinated him. Even an untrained observer like himself could see they were full of anger that the slightest annoyance might unleash.

Suddenly Cherish whipped her head around and grabbed Todd's hand with her mouth. Todd smiled. "That is her way of saying she's had enough petting. She only likes so much and no more. If you noticed, she didn't bite down. Until Amy came that is as far as Cherish would ever go. Now she's just as apt to lash out with her claws. We've thought of declawing her, but she needs them for protection because she slips outside on occasion. Besides, I am afraid she would probably start biting for real if she didn't have her claws."

Margaret made no comment. She stared at the cat, as if sending her a mental message. Cherish settled down on the coffee table, with her feet curled under her and her yellow eyes fixed on Margaret.

When Todd realized the cat was going to stay put, he scooted back and leaned against an upholstered, brown chair. Kate returned and sat in the same chair.

Margaret shifted her gaze from the cat to the Davidsons. She studied them. "I assume the shelter explained how I work."

Kate shrugged. "They said you go into some sort of trance or something."

"No. Not a trance. Animals project feelings and mental images, instead of words, when they communicate psychically. I try to tune into what they are feeling and experiencing. I use a relaxation technique to help me become more inwardly receptive. That's all. I'm in what some might term either a meditative, prayer, passive listening or alpha level state—depending on the describer's belief system. Very relaxed, but alert, would be another way of putting it."

Todd asked, "Similar to the mental state people are often in when watching television?"

"That would be one way of putting it, yes. That is very astute of you to make that connection." She smiled at Cherish. "But we're getting away from the purpose of my being here."

Margaret shifted forward and faced the couple squarely. "There is one thing you need to understand and be prepared for. I am going to give you Cherish's version of the situation. You may not like what I am going to say. All I ask is that you hear the whole thing out before making any comments. Can you do that?"

Husband and wife looked questionably at each other. Todd answered, "We can."

"Good." She leaned back. "Now I am going to relax, then ask Cherish why she has been misbehaving." With back straight and hands palm up on her lap, Margaret went into the same relaxing routine Dan saw her use at Sharon's home. While she took less than five minutes, to the observers the time seemed to tick by slowly. The Davidsons watched Margaret, intrigued. Dan glanced around, bored.

Margaret spoke in a soft monotone. "I have a mental image. Cherish is coming into the living room. She sees her humans sitting on the sofa. They are playing with Amy, who is sitting between them. Cherish senses the love being manifested and wants to be part of it. She jumps into Todd's lap. He pushes her off. 'Get down, Cherish. We're playing with the baby.' Cherish sits on the floor, confused. She can't understand what's happened. She has always been allowed on their laps before. She decides to try again. She jumps into Kate's lap and is rejected. Now Cherish is totally bewildered. She tries a third and a forth time to join them and is rejected each time.

"She quits and curls up in the lounge chair. She watches her humans, trying to understand their reaction to her. She senses the small human has something to do with it. And she doesn't understand her humans' fascination with such a changeable, unpredictable creature."

Margaret halted and sat quietly for a moment. She said, "I am getting a whole series of images," and fell silent again.

The Davidsons and Dan looked at each other, not knowing what to say or do. The mobile home was quiet except for the sound of the furnace kicking on. Cherish yawned.

Margaret opened her eyes, but remained sitting with her back straight. "To summarize, Amy has the run of the house and Cherish can't stay out of her way. Amy invades what Cherish considers her territory. If Cherish tries to eat the packet of moist food that Kate gives her each morning, Amy shows up and bothers her. Several times, when Kate wasn't looking, Amy helped herself to Cherish's food. Cherish tried to tell Kate she was still hungry by crying and rubbing against Kate's legs. Kate said, 'Leave me alone, I'm busy.'

"When Cherish wants a drink of water, Amy is there interfering. At least Kate refilled her water dish without knowing Amy drank from it. She also makes a special effort to keep Amy away from Cherish's litter box, which is some help to Cherish." Margaret glanced at Kate to see how she was reacting. Kate blushed, but remained silent.

Margaret continued. "Amy has one habit that especially angers Cherish. The cat will be curled up asleep in her basket when Amy will suddenly grab her fur with both hands and pull Cherish from her bed. Cherish has hunted for a more secure place to sleep. But every time Cherish thinks she's found a safer place, Amy finds her. If Cherish tries to sleep on higher things, like Todd's desk or the bedroom chest of drawers, either Kate orders her down because she's not supposed to be there or Amy figures a way to climb to where Cherish is. They've developed a reversed version of the old cat and mouse game.

"Cherish knows better than to hurt Amy, but the child's actions are driving her to the raw edge of tolerance. I received one image of Cherish playing with her favorite catnip ball under the kitchen table. She thought Amy was napping. Suddenly, Amy jerked Cherish's tail. Cherish screeched in pain and lashed out in self-defense, striking Amy. Kate came running. When she saw the scratches on the squalling tot's arm, she scolded Cherish. 'How could you hurt a baby?' Cherish hid under the living room chair, watching Kate comfort the child, longing for a little sympathy herself. Her rear throbbed from the yanking Amy gave her.

"The scratching didn't teach Amy anything. Cherish's frustration grew. She tried communicating her unhappiness by refusing to use her litter box. It didn't work. She tried clawing the drapes and furniture in Amy's room. That also didn't work. She grew even more short-tempered."

Margaret stopped and looked sternly at Todd and Kate. She smiled at Cherish, who had moved to Margaret's lap and made herself comfortable. With her eyes on the cat, she spoke to the couple. "Didn't you mention earlier that Cherish gets annoyed when she curls up in you lap to sleep, and you pet her too long?"

Kate answered. "She would warn us to stop, first by wagging her tail. If we didn't respond, she would gently take our hand in her mouth. That usually worked. If we forgot and started petting her again, she would give us a dirty look and jump off our laps."

"That was before Amy moved in and pushed her to the point of exploding?"

Kate blushed. "That's right. Now she is just as likely to lash out with no warning. She has scratched Todd's mother and our minister."

Todd chimed in. "We've warned people to leave her alone, and not let her lie in their laps. Some of them won't listen."

Kate added, "Like Mr. Jones."

"Mr. Jones?"

"Todd's boss. We invited him to dinner one night and…"

Margaret motioned for Kate to stop. "Don't tell me. Let me see if I can get Cherish's version." She exchanged glances with the cat and returned to her meditative posture.

After a moment, she spoke softly. "I see a large man in a business suit seated on the sofa here. Cherish senses his friendly nature, and heads for his lap. By now she is starved for some understanding and caring attention. She is annoyed when Todd starts to remove her from Mr. Jones' lap, and pleased when the stranger insists she be allowed to remain.

"Cherish settles down on Mr. Jones's lap. He strokes her. At first Cherish enjoys the petting. Then, as is her nature, she soon tires of it and wants to rest in his warm lap without being stroked. She gently wags her tail. No one pays attention. Kate is busy in the kitchen. Mr. Jones and Todd are engrossed in conversation. Cherish wags her tail faster. Again no one notices. The rhythm of Mr. Jones' stroking intensifies along with the men's conversation. Cherish lets out a low hiss. It isn't heard. She lays her ears back. Mr. Jones, unknowingly, increases his petting. Cherish's long simmering anger boils over. She lashes out. Mr. Jones grabs his cheek and jumps up, throwing Cherish to the floor. Cherish immediately realizes she has done something wrong and is in trouble. She dashes for the master bedroom and hides under the bed." Margaret opened her eyes and leaned back.

Todd said, "She made three deep scratches that ran from the corner of Mr. Jones' eye to his chin. I felt really terrible about it."

Kate added. "You know. I always thought Cherish gave no warning to Mr. Jones, but if you are correct, she was using body language. She just didn't warn by taking his hand in her mouth as she always did in the past. Mr. Jones was right."

Margaret asked, "How's that?"

Todd explained. "Mr. Jones said it could have been as much our fault as hers. He insisted that she probably tried to communicate a warning, but we were too busy to notice. He was very understanding--probably because he has two cats of his own. Thank God."

Kate spoke up. "Understanding or not. That is when we decided to get rid of Cherish. Next time she may injure someone's eye. And she could really hurt Amy."

"There doesn't have to be a next time." Margaret's gaze shifted from husband to wife and back again, studying them. "What do you think of the information I gave you?"

The couple glanced at each other. Todd cleared his throat. "To be honest, we didn't think you could do what the shelter claimed. But, we felt we owed it to

Cherish to give you a chance. Cherish was a likable, well-behaved cat until Amy came."

"Now what do you think?"

Todd shrugged. "I'm not sure. You were accurate on a lot of details you had no way of knowing, such as what Mr. Jones was wearing and that Kate was in the kitchen."

Kate added, "And that Cherish had a catnip ball and scratched Amy under the kitchen table."

Todd nodded in agreement. "With all that circumstantial evidence, I suppose we really do have to give some credence to what you have told us."

Margaret's smile broadened till her upper lip disappeared. "Good. There is hope for Cherish yet. She leaned toward the couple. "Tell me. What do you think you've learned from hearing Cherish's side?"

Kate and Todd looked at each other, obviously embarrassed. Kate spoke first. "I guess we were so wrapped up in Amy, and all that was involved in adjusting to having a child of our own, that we didn't see what was going on in front of us."

Todd nodded. "That's right. We knew Amy tried to play with Cherish at times. But we just thought it was really cute. It never crossed our minds to consider how Cherish felt about it."

There was a challenge in Margaret's tone as she said, "I wonder how much you really love Amy."

Startled, the couple spoke in unison. "What do you mean?"

"Do you love her enough to give her a hard gift?"

Kate asked, "What type of gift is that?"

"Something of lasting value that can be either difficult to give or painful to receive, or both. Yet once it is accepted and applied can be of immeasurable worth to everyone involved. If you think about it, at times life itself can be a hard gift."

Todd asked, apprehensively, "Just what kind of hard gift do you want us to give to Amy?"

"The gift of understanding where her rights begin and end. Teach her all other living things have rights too—starting with Cherish. Teach her that it is wrong to hurt others. Teach her not only by precept but also by example. Children are natural imitators."

Margaret smiled at Kate. "It won't be easy with a child as active as Amy, who is just starting into the terrible two's. But the extra effort will be worth it. The ability to respect the rights of others is a necessary ingredient for establishing good relationships with family, friends, and work-mates."

The couple contemplated Margaret's words. Kate asked, "What about Cherish? The damage is done?"

"I think it can be undone."

"How?"

"First, protect Cherish until Amy's capable of understanding. Teach Amy the proper way to treat animals. Watch her closely to make sure she is following through when she thinks you aren't looking. Second, pay a little more attention to Cherish's emotional as well as physical needs. She was a good cat for you once, and she can be again with a bit of time, effort, and patience on your part."

A fidgety Dan glanced out the window. "The wind's starting to pick up. We'd better get back to town before the north-south roads blow shut."

As they all stood up, Todd said, "We will certainly take into consideration what you have told us, Mrs. Canfield." He reached for his billfold. "How much do we owe you?"

"Nothing. It wouldn't be right. My gift comes from God. I believe it must be given freely, or it will diminish."

Kate handed Margaret and Dan their coats. "We owe you something for your time and trouble."

"The only reward I want is to hear that Amy and Cherish have learned to live together in peace."

Todd was insistent. "It just wouldn't feel right to not pay you something for your time."

"Since you feel so strongly, give a donation to the shelter. They are always in need of money."

"All right, if that's what you want."

"It is."

Sunlight reflected off the snow, causing Dan and Margaret to squint. Margaret pulled her neck scarf tighter. She said, "The weatherman must have miscalculated. This wind is early by several hours. And it is getting stronger fast."

Too angry to speak, Dan replied with a grunt. Margaret pretended not to notice. He was barely aware of getting into the car, or of Margaret's efforts to maneuver it through the countryside.

On some stretches of road the snow flowed across the road in small powdery streams. On others, gusts of blowing snow abruptly cut visibility in half. Margaret slowed down. The wind intensified. A strong gust shook the big Buick, jarring Dan out of his reverie. Margaret slowed to a crawl.

Dan started to return to his musing, when he felt the car slide on a patch of ice. The Buick buried its left rear in a snowdrift. Margaret spun her wheels. Irritated, Dan slammed the car door shut, jerked a shovel out of the trunk, and dug the car out. Every muscle strained as he pushed the big car back on the road, while Margaret steered. By the time they started again, his exertion had exhausted the brunt of his anger.

As soon as they reached home, Dan headed for Laurie's house. Laurie's mother, Catherine, opened the door. "For heaven sake, Dan. Don't just stand there. Come on in out of the cold."

A fire crackled in the fireplace; their old cocker spaniel was stretched out on a rug in front of the hearth, and Laurie's calico cat was curled up on the sofa. The aroma of fresh baked apple pie drifted from the kitchen. Mrs. Carpenter said, "Let me take your coat. I assume you're here to see Laurie."

"If she's not too busy."

With a matchmaker's gleam in her eye that Dan didn't notice, she said, "I doubt if Laurie would ever be too busy to see you. She's in my workroom. It is off of our bedroom. Just follow the sound of the sewing machine. I was getting ready to make some hot chocolate. Would you like some? Good. I'll bring it in as soon as it is ready. You go on in."

Laurie glanced up. "Hi." She turned the sewing machine off. "This is a pleasant surprise. Let me clear off the rocker so you can sit down." She picked up the top half of a dress and held it in front of her. "I decided to make a summer dress, just to remind myself that this winter has to end sometime. What to you think of this floral print?"

Dan glanced at the pink material with a blue flower print. It was like Laurie, bright and cheerful. He shrugged. "It's nice. I don't know much about dresses."

Laurie gave him a searching look and laid the material on the sewing machine. "Okay, what's on your mind?"

"What makes you think I have something on my mind?"

"I know you. That look says there is something bothering you, and you want to talk about it."

Dan frowned. He wasn't sure he liked Laurie being able to read him so well. Maybe he had made a mistake in coming to see her.

She said, "Come on. What is troubling you?"

Dan gave in. "I went with Margaret on one of her consultations." He described in great detail the visit with the Davidsons.

Laurie listened attentively. When he had finished she said, "Interesting, but just what in particular is bothering you?"

Catherine Carpenter bustled into the room, carrying a tray. "Here is the hot chocolate I promised." She shoved a dessert plate into Dan's hand. "I thought you might like a slice of hot apple pie with whipped cream. Laurie made it." She hurriedly passed out the refreshments, gave Laurie a knowing wink, and left. Laurie blushed in embarrassment.

Dan didn't notice. He took a bite of warm pie and considered just how much he should reveal to her. There were some feelings she wouldn't understand or approve of. He said, "I think part of what's bothering me is guilt."

"Guilt?"

"That's right. I've told you I have a little brother named Mikey, thirteen years younger than me, and eleven years younger than my brother, Rick. Because Mikey was such a late comer, I think the family spoiled him.

"Mikey is the type of kid who is always breaking his toys. Not on purpose. He just plays too rough with them. When he was two, we had a small dog, named Charlie. Mikey played the same way with Charlie. No one thought too much about it. Mikey was just being Mikey.

"Charlie began to growl at him. We'd scold the dog, and he would slink away like he was sorry. Then we'd catch him growling at Mikey again. It never occurred to any of us that Charlie was just trying to keep from being manhandled, the best way he knew how. We didn't like to see Mikey being growled at.

"Charlie began snapping at Mikey. We spanked the dog, but it didn't help. Finally, Charlie bit Mikey, when Mikey was bothering him as he tried to sleep.

"Dad said we couldn't have a dog that would bite children. He never considered the possibility the dog was reacting normally out of self-protection. And that we should have been teaching Mikey to behave instead of the dog. Dad took Charlie to the animal shelter, where he was put to sleep because his history of biting meant no one could adopt him."

"I see," Laurie said sympathetically. "Your visit to the Davidsons made you see Charlie's side of it."

"It wasn't just Charlie. We went through two other dogs the same way, before Mikey matured enough to treat them right."

"Tell me. Is Mikey cute?"

"Is he! You should have seen him when he was little. He had curly blonde hair, the biggest blue eyes you ever saw, and an impish grin that could melt anyone. More than once I remember Mom ordering him to look away, so she could stay angry long enough to scold him properly."

"The Davidson's little girl is cute too, isn't she?"

"That's right. Not in the same way Mikey is. But she is a little charmer. How did you know that?"

"I thought so. Cuteness can be blinding."

"What?"

"I read a psychology article about it once. Whether it is charm in an adult or cuteness in a child, people allow the charm and cuteness to blind them. The adults around both Amy and Mikey were so taken with their baby charms that they were oblivious to the harm being done to their animals. It's very difficult to see past that innocent cuteness to what's really happening."

Dan took in Laurie's deep dimples, dancing dark eyes, and round nose. "I'll try to keep that in mind."

"Why are you grinning?"

"Just thinking of another charmer I know."

"Well, you had better make sure his or her cuteness doesn't blind you so badly you can't see what the true situation is."

Dan struggled to keep from laughing. "I'm trying."

Seeing that he was in a better mood, Laurie decided to switch subjects. "It seems to me that you are starting to accept Margaret's ability to communicate with animals."

Dan's good humor disappeared in a flash. "No way. What made you say that?"

"You're willing to believe what she told the Davidsons."

"I've been around Margaret and her pets long enough to recognize she's good at understanding animal psychology. After seeing Amy, it would be easy for her to figure out the cause of Cherish's bad behavior."

"Why would she want to pretend she was getting the information psychically, if she wasn't?"

"It's a gimmick. She has no degrees in animal psychology, no veterinarian's license, nothing of an official nature that would prove she was an expert. Some people won't listen to another, no matter how knowledgeable they may be, unless they have some sort of official document that proves it. Being self-taught doesn't count with them. Margaret bypasses that problem by pretending she has a special psychic gift. It gets people to listen to her."

"You said Cherish was playing with a toy under the kitchen table when Amy grabbed her tail and she scratched Amy. How could Margaret have known that?"

Dan shrugged. "She's good at making educated guesses. As for Cherish's toy, I saw it under the table when we first arrived. Margaret must have seen it also. She figured out that Cherish liked to play with it there, and made up the rest based on what the Davidsons had already told her."

Laurie let out an exasperated sigh. "What possible motive could Margaret have for lying to people? She won't take money."

"It's an ego trip. Convincing people that she is right makes her feel powerful and important while, at the same time, it helps animals. Having been around good-doers all my life, I can guarantee you. Most of them do it just as much to make themselves feel good as they do to help others. And Margaret is more shyster, than good-doer."

"Well, she did you some good without even knowing it, didn't she? She helped you see how your family had allowed your dogs to be mistreated."

Dan frowned at her, his dark brooding eyebrows joining over his nose. Studying him, she said, "You're mad because Margaret proved to be more right on something than your family, aren't you?"

His face reddened. She had hit too close to the truth. It irked him even more for Margaret to have been right while at the same time committing blasphemy by claiming God was the source of her pretend gift. But he didn't want Laurie to know that. It would only lead to another argument.

She started to continue, "I'll even bet you are mad because…"

He held up a hand and made a stop motion. "Drop the subject now, or we'll both be sorry."

She threw up her hands in surrender. "Okay. Okay. Don't spill your hot chocolate over it." He straightened his cup. She asked, "What would it take to convince you that Margaret isn't putting on an act? That she really does have a gift?"

Dan snorted. "Some situation which demonstrated beyond a doubt to me that she couldn't possibly have known something except by mental communication with an animal. Such a situation isn't possible."

Laurie let out an annoying chuckle. "We'll see."

Dan scowled at her. They got along fine except when the subject of Margaret's gift came up. Then she became totally unreasonable. And preachy. Well, he'd had enough. If he couldn't avoid being around Margaret, he could at least stay away from her defender. It would be best if he took her own advice, and not let her attractiveness affect him any longer.

He sat his cup down. "Look, I've got to go. I finished Margaret's cabinets earlier today. I need to finish mounting them and clean up the mess I left. Then I have to get to work on a paper for my economics class." He took a deep breath. "By the way, I won't be able to walk with you anymore," he lied. "I've got some things to do on campus that requires me to leave earlier and come home later than you. Since our schedules have prevented us from eating lunch together this semester, I guess I won't be seeing you as much for a while."

Laurie's face fell. "Okay," she said weakly. She didn't question him, afraid that she'd start crying and make things worse if she did.

Dan's resolve not to have any more to do with Laurie lasted one week.

Then he made up a feeble excuse about everything clearing up faster than he expected, saying they could resume walking together. He refused to admit, even to himself, that he had found his solo trips to campus far lonelier than he thought possible.

CHAPTER FIVE

Spring weather didn't arrive until the first week of April. The snow melted, birds sang, and seeds sprouted. The smells of earth moist from spring rains and of new growth saturated the air. Dan and Laurie walked home from campus, buoyant with the universal joy of rebirth.

Laurie flitted around Dan like a hummingbird at a feeder. "I forgot to tell you this morning. Sharon and Tom bred Lady again. Her pups will be due in May."

Dan frowned. "Why? Didn't they learn anything from the last litter? What if they wind up with another Sobra? Margaret can't rescue them all."

"Tom likes the extra money from selling AKC registered pups. For an additional dollar, he'll take his chances on getting a loser or two."

"Why doesn't Sharon object? She's the one that has to handle all the extra work involved. It seems to me that she should have the final say."

"Tom is very opinionated, and Sharon doesn't like to create a fuss. When it comes to starting an argument she has as much gumption as a dead fish. Besides, she enjoys playing with the pups. What's the harm in their breeding Lady? They aren't like those irresponsible pet owners I read about."

"How's that?" Dan was sorry as soon as the question popped out of his mouth. He wasn't that interested, and he didn't want to get her started.

"There was a series of newspaper articles a couple of years ago about what happens to the surplus puppies and kittens created by too many people letting their pets breed. Some babies are pushed onto people who really don't want them or given to unfit owners. Some are given to shelters where lots are destroyed because there aren't enough adoptive homes for them. Or they are abandoned in the country where they are killed by other animals, or starve to death because they hadn't been taught to hunt. Farmers can't take care of them because they have all the animals they can handle. Some are given to laboratories where they're used in experiments. Regardless of the disposal method, those people who irresponsibly let their pets breed never witness the suffering they helped create for those poor unwanted kittens and puppies."

Dan chuckled. "You can stop evangelizing any time."

"I'm sorry. I did get carried away, didn't I."

She smiled sheepishly. "I have to confess. I'm not immune to puppy charms. I'm looking forward to playing with Lady's pups. Besides, Tom and Sharon are more caring than those people who let their pets breed haphazardly. They won't let Lady breed with just any dog. It has to be a purebred Lab like her.

"Then they will make every effort to see that their pups get only proper homes. They will pay for advertisements. They will take a pup back if it doesn't work out. And if they do get stuck with another undesirable pup, they'll have it put humanely asleep themselves. They won't push the consequences of breeding Lady onto others."

Laurie reminded Dan of a hunting dog pointing at a stuffed quail. He said, "Look, you're wasting energy trying to convince the already convinced. I believe you. Besides, it's too nice a day to be serious. Let's talk about something else." Impulsively, he asked, "How's your love life?"

Laurie blushed. For the first time since he had met her, she didn't have a quick comeback. She looked searchingly at him, wondering if now was the time to confess how much she cared. Finally, she answered, "On hold. Just on hold." She sighed. "I hope." She arched an eyebrow. "Why?"

Dan pondered. Why had he asked? Then he realized he had been wondering for some time why she didn't seem to be dating as much as she did when they first met. He shrugged. "I wanted to change the subject, and it was the first thing that popped into my head." Her reaction amused and intrigued him. "I'm sorry. Did I embarrass you?"

"Who me? No way," she said unconvincingly. "Just curious, that's all." She twirled around in a circle. "Smell that spring air." She breathed deeply. "It makes me tingle all over. Can't you feel it pulsating with new life? Doesn't it make you want to run, or sing?" Dan laughed. "It feels great after a long hard winter, that's for sure. But it tells me it will soon be time to mow the grass."

Laurie put her hand on her hip and stared at him in disgust. "Sometimes you can be so old mannish. All you ever think about is earning your keep at Margaret's or studying to become a businessman. There *are* other things in life."

"I know." He wanted to pull her to him, brush back the loose strand of her brown, wavy hair, and kiss her warm lips. He twitched her chin instead. "I just don't have the time or resources to get involved with anything else." He looked up in surprise. He hadn't realized they were in sight of home. "Look. There's Margaret sweeping her front porch."

Margaret waved at them. She leaned on her broom and waited for them to reach her. "Dan, if you have time, would you hang my porch swing? I'm getting anxious to sit outside and bask in some of this spring weather."

Dan nodded. "I'll do it as soon as I change clothes." He glanced around for Margaret's black shadow. "Where's Sobra?"

Her upper lip disappeared into her smile. "I purchased a dwarf apple tree this morning. It is in the backyard, waiting for you to help me plant it. I left Sobra carefully circling and sniffing it, trying to figure it out. I decided it was best to leave them alone to get acquainted." As if on clue, Sobra started barking. Margaret's smile vanished. "Something is wrong."

All three threw their things down and raced around the side of the house to the gate. Sobra stood in the center of the yard, with fur on end, barking furiously in the direction of the garage.

Dan caught a glimpse of someone's sleeve on the alley side of the building. He motioned for Laurie and Margaret to stay put. And be still. Using the Carpenter's unfenced yard, he quietly, cautiously circled Margaret's property. With Sobra's excited bark ringing in his ears, and his own heart beating rapidly against his chest, he started to step around the side of the garage. A stick snapped under his foot.

Someone yelled, "Let's get out of here." Dan rounded the garage in time to see two men racing down the alley. He chased after them. The fleeing men separated at the street, disappearing in opposite directions. Dan was glad to give up the chase. The disconcerting thought had flashed through his mind that he wouldn't know how to hold them for the police if he caught up with them.

He joined Margaret and Laurie in inspecting the garage's side door. He ran his fingers over freshly made gouges in the wood. "Looks like they were trying to jimmy the lock. After your late husband's power tools, I suspect."

Laurie was aghast. "In broad daylight?"

Margaret said, "They probably figured no one was home since my car isn't here. I took it to the service station three blocks over for a tune-up. They also didn't realize this is the only day of the week when you two don't have late afternoon classes. Did you get a good look at them, Dan?"

He shook his head. "They ran too fast. I think one of them might have been Bill Saxon, but I can't swear to it."

Margaret sighed. "I've been afraid of this. There has been a series of unsolved robberies lately. A lot of them have been within a ten-block radius of our street. Bill Saxon has always liked to walk through the alleys. I've wondered lately if he wasn't also casing places to steal from."

She smiled at Sobra, who was whining for attention at the back gate. "Sobra is a help, but I'm afraid we need more protection than a dog can provide. Dan, will you install a dead bolt lock on the garage door? And check to make sure the locks on all the windows and doors of both house and garage are in good working order?"

"You bet. If someone took your husband's collection of power tools, I would have a hard time working around here."

"Then it's settled. Now it's time I gave Sobra some well deserved praise and lots of hugs."

Dan secured the house and garage to the best of his ability.

The rest of spring flew by with no more incidents. The regular school year ended. Laurie returned to her usual summer job, working in the dining room of the inn in nearby Indian State Park.

The day before Dan's summer classes were to begin, he helped Margaret deliver several grocery sacks of newspapers she had been saving for Sharon. Sharon invited them to see Lady's four-week-old pups.

Tom had made a large pen by parceling off a third of the big, well-lit basement with wire fencing. They kept the concrete floor of the enclosed area covered with newspapers.

Dan found Laurie sitting in the middle of the pen with eight black Labrador retriever butterballs bouncing around her. He asked, "What are you doing here? I didn't see a car. I thought you were working."

"Mom dropped me on her way to the beauty shop. It's my day off. Ouch!" A puppy had sunk its sharp baby teeth into her canvas sneaker. She loosened the growling puppy's hold. "I didn't want to miss an opportunity to play with the puppies."

Dan grinned. "Suffering from an acute case of cuteness blindness, I see." Laurie stuck her tongue out at him.

Margaret greeted Lady before paying attention to her pups. Feeling her age, Margaret eased herself down on the floor of the pen. Lady rested her head in her lap. Dan and Sharon plopped down on the newspaper-covered floor.

Two puppies grabbed the sleeve of Sharon's sweatshirt. Playing tug-of-war with them, she said, "I have to confess, Margaret. I had a couple of reasons for inviting you to see the pups while you were here."

"I figured that, Sharon, by the shy way you asked us to see them." A growling pup pulled on Margaret's pant leg. She joined in its game by shaking her leg, while addressing Sharon. "Let me guess. You want me to check these babies out to determine if any are timid like Sobra?"

The two puppies pulling on Sharon's sleeve let go. One saw Dan playing with another pup and decided to join them. The other backed up and cocked its head at Sharon. It yapped and wagged its upright tail. Then it leaped at Sharon, reattaching itself to her sleeve. She smiled at the growling, tugging puppy, then answered Margaret. "That is one reason, yes. I'm almost ashamed to admit the other."

"What is it?"

"Lady went into labor on a Saturday morning. It was the same day Tom's grandparents expected the whole family to gather at their summer cabin for their annual spring get-together. The women clean the cabin and stock it with supplies. The men get the two fishing boats out of dry dock, launch them in the lake, and do any other maintenance jobs that need tending. Tom's family has been doing that every spring for over twenty years. They usually do it in April, but this year they couldn't get together until May."

Laurie had been enjoying a growling match with a puppy. She looked up. "Oh, Sharon. You didn't leave Lady alone again?"

Sharon shifted in embarrassment. "I tried to talk Tom out of going. He wouldn't listen. He said Lady could handle the situation alone. That's when I decided to tell him that Margaret had found out what happened to the dead pup in the first litter." She glanced at Margaret. "What he said isn't fit for repeating. Let's just say he didn't believe you. He insisted animals always know what to do. They never need supervision."

Margaret sighed. "So how many pups did you find dead when you returned home."

"Two."

Margaret looked sadly at the black butterball tugging on her pant leg. "Now you want me to find out what happened."

"If you wouldn't mind."

"All right. It may do some good. Though I doubt it."

Dan's spirits had sunk as he listened to their conversation. Had he known Sharon was going to ask Margaret to display her "gift" he would have stayed home. He wanted no part of her fooling people with her perverted form of help. Besides, Margaret had promised she wouldn't ask him to go along on a consultation unless it was an emergency.

He glanced at Margaret, who was watching him. She shrugged her shoulders in a "I'm sorry. It can't be helped" gesture. He resigned himself to the inevitable.

Margaret struggled to her feet. "The first thing we need to do is to see what sort of dispositions these pups have." She looked apologetically at Dan, who was detaching a pup from his shirtsleeve. "Dan, would you and Laurie take Lady upstairs." She turned to Sharon. "I want all the puppies put outside the pen so we can keep the checked separated from the unchecked. I'll stay inside the pen. You hand me the pups one at a time. That way I can get a feel for each individual's personality."

Dan took his time getting to his feet. He was enjoying playing with the puppies and didn't want to quit. Besides, he wasn't looking forward to watching Margaret's pretend act with Lady.

He reluctantly handed the first pup over the wire fence to Sharon. Suddenly he realized that his foot felt strangely warm.

A male puppy was piddling on his white tennis shoe.

A flustered Sharon said, "Oh, I'm sorry, Dan." She stood there, repeating, "I'm sorry. I'm sorry."

Laurie found some paper toweling for him. He glanced at Sharon. "It's okay." He grinned at Laurie. "I think I just discovered one of the hazards of cuteness blindness." She shot him a dirty look.

Dan's foot felt cold and slushy by the time he reached the kitchen. Laurie proceeded to make a pitcher of ice tea. He removed his sock and laid it across the top of his shoe. Lady sniffed it, then laid down beside it. Laurie handed him a glass of tea. He eyed her as she sat down at the table. "You and Sharon aren't at all alike, are you?"

"What makes you say that?"

"The different ways you reacted when the pup wet on my shoe, for one. For another, I get the feeling if you'd been in Sharon's position when Lady went into labor, you would have insisted Tom either go by himself to his family gathering or find someone to stay with Lady—regardless of how much ranting and raving he did. It's my guess if you believe something isn't right, there's no way anyone is going to force you to do it—short of holding a gun on you."

Laurie laughed. "True. Dad always said I had all the nerve, and Sharon all the timidness. When he would get mad at one of us, he'd wave his arms and say, 'I wish I could put you two in a bag and shake it so you'd come out more even." She turned thoughtful. "Sometimes, when I see how lopsided Sharon and Tom's relationship is when it comes to making decisions, I wish Dad could have."

Sharon popped out of the basement doorway, with Margaret trailing. Beaming, Sharon said, "Guess what. Margaret says there isn't a timid one in the whole bunch. Tom will be happy." She frowned. "Of course, he'll have to figure it out for himself. He'd never believe it just on Margaret's say-so. I won't tell him anyway. He'd scold me if he knew I had asked her to check them."

Laurie and Dan gave each other a knowing look. Dan chuckled. He imagined someone trying to scold Laurie as if she were a child. It would be like putting a fire under a gas can. He wouldn't want to be near when she exploded. Still, he had to admit he admired her spunk.

Margaret glanced at her watch. "It's getting late. Let's take Lady in the living room where we can all get comfortable."

Carrying his shoe and sock, Dan reluctantly limped after the women.

It didn't take Margaret long to begin speaking in the quiet monotone she used when speaking from an alpha level. "I have the scene. A large cardboard box is lying on its side, lined with shredded newspapers." She opened her eyes and glanced at Sharon. "This whelping box was smaller than the one used with the first litter, wasn't it?"

"That's right. We couldn't find a box as big as the first one. Tom thought about not using a box at all.

Then our vet told him that dogs need a feeling of cave-like protection when giving birth. The box we used was for a cabinet model television."

Margaret said, "That would've been adequate under the right conditions."

She looked at her watch. "I'm in a bit of a hurry. I'll pick up the images, if I can. Then give you the shortened version." She closed her eyes, straightened her back, and took a deep breath. After a moment, she said, "I have the scene." She fell silent. Dan and the sisters waited.

Margaret opened her eyes and leaned back against the sofa. "Lady's second labor was far more strenuous than the first. Each succeeding pup took longer to be born. Lady constantly shifted around in the box, trying to get comfortable. The pain was excruciating at times. The sixth pup was especially difficult in coming. Lady was so engrossed in her struggle, she forgot about the five newborns scattered around her in the crowded box. As she was pushing to get the sixth pup out, she unknowingly trapped one of the tiny babies between her body and the box. It suffocated. After she cleaned the sixth pup, she collapsed from exhaustion. She slept until intense labor pains woke her. That's when she discovered she had lain on a second helpless newborn, crushing it to death with her weight."

Unshed tears floated in Sharon's pale eyes. "The box *was* too small."

Margaret shook her head. "Lady could have laid on a pup even in a bigger box, if it just happened to be in the wrong spot at the time."

"I guess it couldn't have been helped then."

Margaret leaned forward with an angry, matriarchal glare. "Look. You and Tom do a fair job of caring for Lady and her pups. You make sure they have proper nutrition, good veterinary care, and a decent exercise area. When the pups are old enough, you take proper responsibility for seeing they get homes. However, there are areas where you are lacking. The biggest are breeding Lady for the wrong reasons and failing to supervise her labors."

"But Tom…"

"Don't Tom me! If it were you giving birth, you can bet he'd want someone there to help. He wouldn't leave you alone just because birthing is a natural process. He knows things can go wrong when a human baby is born. Well, things can go wrong with animals also. Even wild ones. If you're going to breed Lady, either be *completely* responsible for her and her babies welfare, or don't breed her."

Sharon hung her head. "What could we have done if we had stayed home?"

"You could have moved those helpless, blind babies away from Lady when she was in the throbs of deepest labor. Then, after she'd cleaned the newest one, you could have given them back to her to continue the bonding between mother and infants until the next birth was imminent. You could have done that between each birth."

"But Tom wouldn't…"

"Tom's just bull-headed; he's no monster. He wouldn't have beaten you or verbally abused you if you'd insisted on staying home that day. You've got a mind and will of your own. Use them. My guess is that Tom might even respect you a little more if you'd occasionally take a stand for what you believe in. Then your marriage would be a true partnership instead of the parent-child drivel it is now."

Sharon burst into tears. Margaret was taken aback. "I'm sorry, Sharon. I'm afraid I got carried away. I had no right to jump you so badly. It's just hard for me to see animals suffer needlessly to satisfy some selfish desire for extra pocket money or to play with the babies." Margaret shifted to the arm of Sharon's chair, hugged Sharon, and let her cry on her shoulder.

Sharon blew her nose. "It's okay, Margaret. I don't blame you for being upset with us." She shook her head weakly. "But there is no clear right or wrong way in this situation. And it's just not as simple with Tom as you think."

Margaret sighed. "Perhaps not. But I would at least think about it if I were you." She glanced at her watch and stood up. "Dan, we've got to go. I have a dental appointment, and I have to drop you off at home first."

While Dan put on his damp, smelly shoe and sock, Margaret hugged both sisters good bye. She asked, "How are the invitations and plans for the Fourth of July coming? Will Dan and I see you both there?"

Laurie answered. "Mom has everything arranged. But I won't be able to go to the picnic area. I have to work at the inn."

Sharon said, "Tom and I'll be there." She added excitedly, "So will Robert. He's coming home on a short leave."

"Really? That's wonderful. It will be good to see him."

Dan stood up, testing the feel of his damp shoe. "I'm ready."

A gentle breeze ruffled Dan's chestnut hair as they left the house. The bright sunshine forced him to use his hand as an eyeshade, as he waited for Margaret to unlock the car door. Still feeling miffed at being forced to watch Margaret's performance, he asked, "Do you think your little act did any good?"

Margaret was startled at his choice of words, but didn't answer. She waited until they had settled into the car and put their seat belts on. "Probably not. It's going to take a lot more than talking to get Sharon to accept responsibility when Tom won't. In some ways I hold her more accountable than Tom. He's acting out of ignorance and misplaced pride. She knows better." Margaret turned her attention to maneuvering the car through the suburb full of playing children.

Dan pondered the cleverness of Margaret's act. Guessing the whelping box was smaller than the first was a stroke of genius. If he wasn't absolutely convinced psychic communication with animals was impossible, he would be tempted to believe her himself. With Margaret's dignified carriage and ladylike manner, it would be hard for anyone, who even remotely entertained the idea of psychic ability, not to believe her. He was glad he was smart enough not to seriously consider the idea, even for a second.

For the first time, he understood how Laurie could be taken in so easily. If that were the only problem, he would drop his concerns and consider getting more involved with Laurie some day. But she had also swallowed Margaret's heretical beliefs. That he couldn't ignore because of the teachings of his mother's church.

Margaret pulled up in front of her house. As Dan opened the car door, he remembered something she had said to the Carpenter sisters. "What was that about seeing us on the Fourth of July?"

"I guess I forgot to tell you. The Carpenter clan is having a reunion picnic at Indian State Park on the Fourth. We've been invited to join them."

"Is the Robert that Sharon mentioned their brother who is a career officer in the army?"

"That's right. He is a lieutenant, but I hear he is about to be promoted to captain. He hasn't been home for two years. Look, I've got to get going or I'll be late. We'll talk about it later."

"Okay."

The Fourth of July was hot and dry. The motionless air felt stuffy in both woods and open areas of the park. Dan estimated that there were at least seventy-five Carpenter related adults and children. Women puttered around the tables in the open-sided shelter. The older men sat in lawn chairs talking sports. Laurie's father, Frank, worked at the grill. Children swarmed everywhere.

Margaret had made sure Dan and Robert were properly introduced. Dan would have known Robert anywhere. He had Laurie's ash brown hair and dark eyes. Robert invited Dan to join him in fishing off the shaded bank of nearby White River, which flowed through the park woods.

They had been fishing for an hour when Tom strolled up. "Having any luck?"

Robert motioned for him to sit down. "Just little stuff. No keepers. Want to try? I have an extra pole."

"No, thanks. I'll just watch."

Dan reeled in a small sunfish, unhooked it, and tossed it back into the river. "How are the pups?"

Tom laughed. "Great. They're all spoken for. I'll make a nice little profit from this litter. You know, when I decided to get a registered Labrador retriever, I only wanted it to try my hand at hunting. I wasn't sure I even wanted a female. But the breeder said Lady was the best of the litter. I'm glad he talked me into taking her." He smiled slyly. "I wasn't going to breed her, but a friend said it was good for her to have sex. Then I learned if both parents are registered purebreds like Lady, you can make some money selling the pups. That beats hunting any day. I'll breed her again as soon as she comes into heat again. That should be in about four months."

"You're what!" They turned to find Margaret glaring down at Tom from the top of the bank. Dan had never seen her look so angry, not even when she had scolded Sharon. All three young men shrank from her stare. "Tom, did I hear you correctly? Are you planning to breed Lady when she comes into heat again?"

"That's right," Tom answered defiantly.

"You can't do it. That last labor was too hard on Lady. She needs time to regain her strength. No dog should be allowed to breed with every heat."

"Wild members of the dog family breed every time they come into heat."

Margaret's anger deepened. "Most wild canines have only one heat a year. Domesticated dogs have been bred to have two. Breeding them that close together is as draining on them as it is for a woman to have a baby every year. If you care for Lady at all, you won't put her through it."

Tom glanced at Dan and Robert, embarrassed at their witnessing this. His face reddened. He leaped to his feet and headed up the bank. "You have no right to speak to me like that. Lady's mine and I know what's best for her." He marched past her. Suddenly, he spun around. "Besides, I love Lady. And you know it." Without waiting for a reply, he headed back up the path to the picnic area.

Margaret watched his retreat until he disappeared into the woods. She turned to Dan and Robert. "It's true," she said. "He does care deeply for her. Unfortunately, like a lot of people, ignorance and greed control his actions more than compassion—even for loved ones."

She snapped her fingers. "I almost forgot. I came to let you know that the food is ready."

Robert said, "Good. I'm starved." He grabbed his pole and started reeling in his line. "We'll be there as soon as we store our gear in the car." With obvious admiration, he watched Margaret as she strolled back up the path. "Margaret is an amazing woman. She still cares as deeply for people as she does for animals, even after all the cruelty she's seen and the hurt people have given her personally."

Dan cut the hook off his line and placed it in Robert's tackle box. "What kind of hurt?"

"It's been mostly connected with her gift. She's been called every nasty thing you can imagine. She's even been accused of conspiring with the devil. But, it isn't casual acquaintances that have hurt her the most. Her son, Calvin, managed that."

"I have wondered about him. Margaret never mentions him, and I've noticed they don't communicate with each other."

"That is the way Calvin wants it. He was embarrassed by Margaret's gift when he was growing up. His schoolmates teased him, sometimes unmercifully. As soon as Calvin graduated from college, he found a job as far away from home as he could get. From then on, he kept his contacts to a minimum. "After his father died, he cut off communication completely. Did you ever hear of anything so dumb?"

Dan felt his face reddening. His sympathies were with Calvin. Instead of answering, he started grabbing up the gear. Robert helped him. They left the lukewarm woods and headed for the hot parking lot.

Robert asked, "Did you know that Margaret has two grandchildren she has never seen and probably never will?"

"No. I didn't."

"That's her greatest grief. She doesn't discuss it, but my family has noticed her watching children their ages. Sometimes she has tears in her eyes."

"Your family has known Margaret for a long time, haven't they?"

"Since before I was born. Now her husband is gone and most of her other relatives live too far away, are dead, or ignore her. That's why our family adopted her as an honorary Carpenter, and invited her to this picnic."

Robert unlocked the car trunk and tossed the fishing gear in. He wiped his sweaty forehead. "Dan, are you aware Margaret regards you as another son?"

Dan stared at him in astonishment. "You're kidding! I have always considered our relationship a straight up front business-only arrangement." He saw no reason to mention how hard he worked to keep it that way.

"That's not the way Margaret sees it. I heard her tell Mother that you reminded her of Calvin. You have the same body build. Both of you were taught by your fathers to be handy with tools and are gung-ho on business careers. She feels she has been given a second chance with you."

Robert's good-nature smile disappeared. "I thought it might be a good idea for you to know that." He studied Dan intently. "I'd hate to think you would do anything to hurt her the way Calvin did."

Dan suddenly felt hotter than the July heat. He shifted uncomfortably.

Noting his embarrassment, Robert said, "What the heck." He grinned and swung his arm around Dan's shoulder. "All negative talk should be outlawed on holidays. This is a day for fun, and we're going to have it. But first, let's get some food."

"Okay." But Dan's holiday mood was gone for good.

CHAPTER SIX

Dan barely noted the arrival of cooler, fall days. He carried an extra heavy class load and was too busy trying to keep his grades up to bother with the splendor of autumn in Indiana. He did notice—only because he had to rake them—that the leaves fell like colorful snowflakes with every breeze.

One crisp evening Margaret took Sobra for a walk after supper. Dan sat in his room, cramming for a test in business law. Taylor slept in his usual spot on Dan's desk. The wind picked up and tapped a tree limb against the window, distracting Dan. Making a mental note to trim the branch tomorrow, he tried his best to ignore it and concentrate on his class notes.

He had almost succeeded in immersing himself in his studies when, suddenly, Taylor let out a piercing screech and leaped to his paws. Dan jumped, knocking his notes off the desk. His heart felt like it was pounding to get out. "Taylor! You nearly scared me witless."

Dan scooped up his papers. "I've probably forgotten everything I just learned."

Taylor gave out a pleading meow. His yellow eyes implored Dan to do something.

"What is the matter with you?" Dan picked the old cat up and examined him as thoroughly as he knew how. "I can't find a thing wrong with you. Maybe you had a bad dream." He put the cat on his towel. "Go back to sleep and let me study."

Taylor dashed back to Dan's open textbook, sat on it, looked Dan full in the face, and meowed. Dan snorted in disgust. "Look, I don't have time for you. I've got a big test tomorrow."

He grabbed the cat by the scruff of the neck and deposited him on the floor. Taylor planted his claws in Dan's jeans, stared up at him, and cried beseechingly. Dan carefully eased the old cat's claws out of his pant leg.

"Look, Taylor. I don't know what you want. The bedroom door is open so you can leave. Your food, water, and litter box are in their usual places downstairs. And I gave you plenty of attention before I sat down to study. You never go outside, so I know that isn't what you want. You should be the most contented cat in the world."

Taylor reached up and dug his claws in Dan's thigh. Dan leaped up. "That does it." He dumped Taylor in the hallway and slammed the door. Taylor let out a wail Dan felt sure was capable of waking every cat in every pet cemetery across the country. Dan sat with elbows on his desk, hands over his ears, trying to decide what to do. He just had to get some studying done.

He heard the front door fly open. Margaret shouted up the stairs. "Dan! I need you!" Man and cat raced down the stairs and into the kitchen. Sobra was gulping down her water. Margaret was rummaging in a drawer.

She held up a flashlight. "Quick, come with me. Something has happened to Katy."

Dan grabbed his jacket from the pantry. Margaret opened the backdoor. Taylor streaked out. Dan froze in astonishment as Taylor vanished into the darkness. Dan couldn't believe it. That old feline had as much of an aversion to the outdoors as most humans did to eating earthworms.

Margaret pulled on Dan's jacket sleeve. "Don't just stand there. Let's get going."

It was a black, chilling evening. The gusting wind was the harbinger of an approaching storm. Falling leaves swirled in the air around them. Margaret's flashlight played back and forth across the ground like a beacon. They stopped under a streetlight at the end of the alley.

Margaret yelled, "Katy." She stopped to listen; she had taught her cats to respond when she called. "Katy." There was no answering meow. "Katy!" The wind rattled an empty, metal trashcan. "Katy!"

Margaret stood still and closed her eyes. She took several deep breaths in an effort to quiet herself. Her eyes flew open. "It's no use, Dan. I'm too worried and flustered. I can't calm my mind enough to pick up on her psychically. We're going to have to search the neighborhood. I only have one flashlight. You search the areas lit by streetlights. Sobra and I will scour the darker areas."

They combed a four-block area, calling, stopping to listen, and straining to hear an answering meow above the wind. They ended up in front of Margaret's house. Trying to hold down her wind whipped hair, she said, "My cats never go out of earshot of home. Katy must be unconscious, or worse."

They stood there, wondering what to do next. Barely audible, a cat meowed in the distance. Margaret straightened. "That's Taylor. He's found her." She yelled above the wind, "Taylor!" He answered. She yelled, "Keep talking, Taylor. We're coming." She kept calling, using his wind distorted responses for a guide.

They found Taylor in some thick bushes that ran along the alley behind Saxon's property. Taylor was circling, sniffing a box-shaped contraption. Three sides were covered with screen wire. The fourth side was made of heavy wood. Unconscious, Katy was squeezed between the solid side and a heavy wooden panel fastened to it. It took both Margaret, holding the box steady, and Dan, pulling, to get the panel to lift against the powerful springs holding it against Katy. Dan labored to keep the panel up while Margaret carefully eased Katy out of the way. Dan let go. The panel snapped shut, knocking the whole devise backward two feet.

Dan held the flashlight while Margaret examined the gray cat. He nodded toward the box, his voice tense with anger. "Did you get a close look at that contraption? There is a live mouse in it. Someone deliberately set a trap designed to crush a cat or small dog." He glanced toward Bill Saxon's darkened house. "It's not hard to figure out who did it." He saw Margaret had finished her examination. "How is she?"

"She's still alive. Let's get her to the vet. Go get a piece of plywood, and a blanket. And bring the car around here."

Dan grabbed up the trap. "I'm going to make sure this thing doesn't hurt another animal." Taylor led the way as he headed back to the house.

They slid the board carefully under Katy. Lifting it together they carried it toward the car, walking slowly to keep from jarring and causing further damage to the unconscious cat. Margaret said, "As soon as I can, I'm going to consult Sergeant Beacon."

"Who is Sergeant Beacon?"

"He's a police officer who does volunteer work at our shelter. He won't be able to do anything officially without definite proof as to who did this, but he can advise me on what to do. If Bill did set this trap, you can bet there is going to be more in the future."

Later that evening, heavy rain pounded Margaret's house. Dan sat, warm and dry, at the kitchen table, drinking hot chocolate, and waiting for Margaret to get off the telephone. Taylor jumped into his lap. Dan smiled and scratched the old cat's head. Until he saw Katy, hurt and unconscious, in that trap, Dan hadn't realized how effectively Taylor had taught him to appreciate cats.

Margaret strolled into the kitchen, trailed by Sobra and Princess. "That was the vet. Katy has three broken ribs, a punctured lung, and a concussion; but he thinks she is going to make it. He should know for sure in a day or two."

"That's great." He stroked Taylor, who purred. "Do you know that Taylor here was acting like something was wrong before you came into the house?"

"It doesn't surprise me. He probably sensed Katy was in trouble the same as I did. Though he is almost seventeen years old, he is still the most psychic of all the animals I have ever had over the years. That's why he reacted while Sobra and Princess didn't."

Dan stared at her, wide-eyed. "What do you mean you *sensed* Katy was in trouble?"

Margaret took a sip of hot chocolate, then shrugged. "ESP, extrasensory perception."

Dan decided to play along. "I thought you had to be in the presence of an animal to communicate with it."

"It is easier for me when I am working with other people's pets. But it isn't absolutely necessary."

"You're saying that you somehow picked up psychically from Katy that she was in trouble?"

"Not totally. Animals communicate with nonverbal images. If it had been straight mind to mind from Katy, I would have gotten an image of what she was sensing or seeing. That is why I don't take lost pet cases. My success rate is low because the lost animal can't project a specific enough image for me to know where to look. I can only see it from their angle. The few times I've been successful were when either the pet's owner or I recognized the place I was seeing. And the odds of that happening are slim. No, this time I just got an overpowering feeling that Katy was in trouble."

"Couldn't you have, without realizing it, heard her cry out in a normal way before she passed out?"

"Hardly. Sobra and I were walking near the elementary school when I realized Katy was in trouble. That's four blocks away."

"Maybe the wind carried the sound."

"The wind was blowing in the opposite direction."

Dan frowned, trying to figure it out. There has to be a logical explanation other than extrasensory perception. There just has to be. He suddenly remembered declaring to Laurie that it would take a situation where it was impossible for Margaret to have known something except psychically to convince him her gift was real. He sat, holding his cup motionless in midair. You don't suppose. No! It couldn't be. There just has to be another explanation.

Dan gulped down the last of his hot chocolate so fast he choked. Between coughs, he said, "I've got to get back upstairs. I've got some thinking—I mean studying—to do."

The next morning found everything soaked from the night's storm. The weather was beginning to clear and warm up as Dan and Laurie strolled towards the campus. Laurie watched him, puzzled. "You're unusually quiet this morning. Is something wrong?"

"No," Dan lied. "I'm trying to review some material in my head for a test in business law."

"Oh. In that case, I won't bother you." She walked silently by his side.

Dan was grateful. He was in too great a state of confusion to talk. He hadn't slept or studied since last night's episode. He couldn't get Margaret's knowing about Katy off his mind. If he accepted Margaret's gift as genuine, then he would have to move out. It meant his mother's beliefs were closer to the truth than he had thought. Living with a shyster was one thing, but living with someone possessing evil powers was another matter all together.

On the other hand, if Margaret's abilities weren't evil—which was highly unlikely—it would crack the very foundations of his beliefs about the nature of man, animal, and life. Man was man. Animals were animals, and valueless in and of themselves. Their only worth came from the use man made of them.

If it was possible for Margaret's gift to be genuine, but not evil, then what he had been taught about the perceptional and soul qualities of both man and animal was in question. He might even have to rethink his religious convictions. He shrank inwardly from that thought. He couldn't stand to go through *that* again.

His father was raised a middle-of-the-road Methodist. But his mother was raised in and spent her entire life belonging to a small, independent church that was strict fundamentalist. They put a lot of emphasis on fighting evil and sin. When Dan grew old enough to be baptized into her church, she pressured him into doing so.

He loved his mother and wanted to please her. However, for two years after his baptism, he suffered inner turmoil trying to force himself to believe the same as his mother and her church. It wasn't until he finally rejected their beliefs as too fanatical and accepted his father's more lenient views, that he found a certain level of peace. And, like his father, he did not feel a need for a church.

Dan wanted nothing to do with anyone or anything that might shake or destroy that peace. No. The only acceptable explanation was that Margaret lied. But, if that was the case, how *did* she know Katy was in trouble? His mind whirled and whirled in endless circles."

The blaring of an automobile horn jarred Dan out of his reverie. A compact car pulled over to the curve on the opposite side of the street. A young man leaned across and rolled down his passenger side window. He yelled at Dan. "Don't you live with Mrs. Canfield?"

Dan eyed him, suspicious as to who this stranger could be. He nodded a reluctant yes. "Why do you want to know?"

The stranger smiled. "You don't remember me, do you?"

"No. I'm sorry. I've been distracted this morning. My memory isn't working like it should."

"That's okay. I understand. We can all get like that at times. I'm Todd Davidson. You and Mrs. Canfield visited us last winter when we were having trouble with our cat, Cherish."

"I remember now. How are things going?"

"Great. That is what I wanted to tell you. I've been aiming to call Mrs. Canfield, but it keeps slipping my mind. Lucky for me, I had to take a detour this morning and saw you. Will you give Mrs. Canfield a message? Tell her we took her advice. Cherish is her old self again. She is even starting to like Amy, now that Amy is learning how to treat her. Thank Mrs. Canfield again for us."

"I will." Dan felt disgusted as he watched Todd ease his car back into traffic. He didn't appreciate having Todd add to his confusion by reminding him that even if Margaret was evil, her deception could reap good results.

He hiked the rest of the way to campus in such a foul mood that a baffled Laurie hung back, giving him space. They went in opposite directions, without saying good-bye, when they reached the edge of campus.

Dan remained in a mental fog all through his morning classes. He could think of nothing but Margaret and Katy. There has to be a logical explanation he could accept. He took his business law examination at 11:00 a.m. He knew as he handed in his papers that he had ruined his B+ average. That finally gave him the impetus to shove his worries to the back of his mind and concentrate in the rest of his classes.

As he left his last class of the day, someone called his name. Ted Green and Kevin Hartley, two senior business students, were standing in the hallway. A third man, unknown to Dan, stood with them.

Ted placed his hand on the stranger's shoulder. "This is Bob Webster, Dan. He is a graduate student who works in the Dean's office. He was updating the business students' files when he noticed your address. He wanted to meet you. Your landlady is Professor Canfield's widow, isn't she?"

"That's right." He didn't like the amusement in their expressions. "It's strictly a business arrangement."

Ted said, "I'm sure it is. But we've been wondering. Are the rumors about her true?"

Dan's throat went dry. He asked guardedly, "What rumors?"

Bob shot an annoyed glance at Ted and Kevin. He smiled at Dan. "That she claims she can talk to animals and they'll answer back."

Ted grinned. "Does she moo like a cow?"

Kevin laughed. "I'll bet she barks at her cat and meows at her dog. How does she talk to you Dan? Cluck, cluck?"

Dan stiffened with anger. Bob frowned at Ted and Kevin. "Lay off guys." He turned to Dan. "Seriously, I've read about such psychic abilities. Can Mrs. Canfield really communicate with animals? What kind of animals can she communicate with? How did she develop her ability?"

A voice spoke from down the hall. "Good afternoon, gentlemen." Dr. Smead, head of the business department, stood frowning in his office doorway. He tapped his watch. "Have you forgotten you requested a meeting with me that was scheduled to begin five minutes ago?"

The three were immediately apologetic. "Sorry, sir. We're coming, sir."

Bob patted Dan on the shoulder as he passed him. "Maybe we will have the chance to continue this conversation some other time." He hurried after the other two men.

Dan wandered outdoors, disgusted. Now, on top of everything else, Margaret was proving to be an embarrassment. Ted and Kevin had made him feel like a fool. There was no way he could leave the issue shoved to the back of his mind. He would have to make a decision.

He drifted toward the comforting little park at the core of the campus where he had found solace before. He plopped down on a bench covered with leaves still wet from last night's storm. Deep in thought, he was unaware of the brisk wind, the concrete bench, or that the seat of his pants was getting soaked.

"Dan." Laurie stood before him, her dark eyes troubled. "I got worried when you didn't show up at our meeting place. Are you all right?"

'I'm fine." He looked at his watch. "I just lost track of time, that's all." He stood up. "Come on. Let's go."

Laurie's laughter stopped him. She pointed to his seat. "It looks like time isn't the only thing that got away from you."

Dan's face felt as hot as his rear did cold. The nipping wind wasn't helping matters. He tried to pull his jacket down. It was too short. A couple strolled by, grinning at him. The girl giggled. All of a sudden, Margaret's house seemed as far away as Asia.

Laurie said, "Give me your books. You hold your notebook behind you with both hands." She chuckled when he started to move. "Try not to walk so stiff-legged. Act natural."

Dan crossed the campus as quickly as he could manage. Laurie tried, unsuccessfully, to hide her grin behind the stack of books she carried. Dan eyed everyone he passed, wondering if they noticed. All he got were a few puzzled looks. He relaxed when he reached the first nearly empty residential street.

Laurie switched from amused to concerned. "It's probably none of my business, Dan. But what's troubling you so much that you could sit on wet leaves without even realizing it?"

He sighed. "You'll have to know sooner or later, so it might as well be now." He steeled himself. "I've decided to move out of Margaret's place."

"What!" For a brief moment panic played across Laurie's features. She studied him while trying to regain her composure. "How can you? Financially, I mean."

"First, I'll find the cheapest place to live that I can. Then, I'll apply for any available scholarships. If that doesn't work, I'll apply for a college loan. Now that I've proven I can do college work, and am no longer on probation, I should be able to qualify. If I can't get a scholarship or loan, then I guess I'll just have to get a full-time job and reduce my class load. One way or the other, I'll finish my education. You can count on that. It just may take longer than I planned, that's all."

"But why? What's happened to cause you to make such a drastic decision all of a sudden?"

"Okay." He stopped and faced her. "You might as well know the truth." He told her of his encounter with the three students. "I never could stand being made fun of. I won't risk more of it by staying connected with Margaret any longer. It's too embarrassing." He started walking again.

Laurie had to increase her stride to keep up with him. "You mean you're going to hurt Margaret just to guarantee you won't get teased? Either I don't know you as well as I thought or there is more to it than that. Come on. Out with it."

Dan scowled at her, annoyed she had read him so well. He glanced around the quiet residential street, as if looking for something to distract their conversation.

"I'm going to pester you, Dan, until you tell me. So you might as well get it over with."

"You won't like it. And it is for sure you won't agree with me."

"Try me. What is it?"

"Okay, you asked for it." He filled her in on last night's episode with Katy. He ended by saying, "I just can't handle the weirdness anymore."

"So it has finally happened," Laurie said weakly. "I knew it had to sooner or later."

"What?"

"You saw Margaret use her gift in a manner you can't explain away to your satisfaction. Now you've decided if you can't dismiss it any other way, you'll run away from it."

Dan shouted, "I'm not running away. It is just time for me to move out. That's all."

"Nonsense. What is the whole truth? Come on out with it."

"All right. If you must know. I don't want to have anything more to do with Margaret because her gift is evil."

"What!"

"I'll admit it. She *did* prove to me last night that she possesses psychic powers. But all such powers are of the devil."

"That is the biggest bunch of hogwash I have ever heard."

"My mother's church claims that the Bible says…"

Laurie interjected, "The Bible condemns only certain types of psychics. Mainly those who call up the dead and those who try to cast spells, etc. The types that attribute authority and power to a living person or an entity on the other side instead of to God. There are plenty of other forms of psychic phenomenon that the Bible sanctions. Such as psychic dreams, visions, prophesying, healing, speaking in tongues, and so on and so forth. Most of the prophets and disciples displayed extrasensory perceptions that proved their connection to the divine Spirit. As did Jesus. It's the *way* it's developed and used that makes it bad or good."

"Huh! And just how is a person to know when it is being used for evil instead of good? And if it is coming from God or the devil?"

"Use Jesus' standard. Judge it by the fruits of the spirit. Have you ever seen any evidence that Margaret used her gift in a way that resulted in arrogance, unkindness, intolerance, and so on? Have you ever seen anything but good come from her use of her gift?"

"No. But that doesn't mean anything. Haven't you ever heard of a wolf in sheep's clothing? A lot of dishonest characters are expert at tricking people by appearing to be nice and doing God's work. You taught me yourself that charm and cuteness can blind a person to what's really happening."

"All right. You've got a point. But time and careful observation will eventually reveal the truth. Wouldn't it be better to stick around and take the chance, rather than risk throwing away an opportunity to learn something that might be for your and everyone else's higher good?"

"No!"

Laurie threw up her hands. "You are impossible. Maybe you ought to…"

"I don't want to talk about it anymore. You've been too brainwashed by Margaret."

"Okay. Okay."

Dan plodded along, confused. Could he be throwing away an opportunity from God? If so, a lot of what he has accepted as truth was out of kilter. Suddenly, he remembered his promise to his mother not to let anything change him. He clung to the thought as if it was a life preserver. He must not forget his vow.

Laurie waited until they reached their street. "Now that you've had a little more time to think, have you changed your mind about moving?"

"No. Margaret is still way too spooky. I can't stand the idea of living with her a minute longer."

They reached Margaret's house. The cold breeze had dried Dan's pants, though his undershorts still felt damp. "I'll take my books now."

Laurie handed them to him. Her eyes were sorrowful, pleading. "Isn't there anything that will change your mind?"

It struck Dan for the first time that a move would end their walks together. They seldom ate lunch together because of conflicting schedules. With no car or extra money, there would be little opportunity to see Laurie again. He started to melt. Then he remembered last night's episode and her defense of Margaret.

He stiffened. "No. There is nothing, absolutely nothing, that can change my mind." He pointed to Margaret's front door. "I'm going in there right now and tell Margaret. Then I'm going to start calling around to find a place."

Tiny pools of tears formed in Laurie's dark eyes, threatening to spill down her cheeks. Fearful of losing control himself, Dan whirled around and marched stiffly up to Margaret's door. He glanced back to discover Laurie still standing where he had left her, watching him. In an uncertain tone, he said, "I'll be seeing you." She nodded sadly and turned toward her house.

Dan threw open the door and yelled, "Margaret." A muffled answer came from the side room, originally designed for a parlor, that Margaret called her second living room. To keep his courage going, Dan continued to talk as he advanced toward the room and unseen woman. "I've got something I need to tell you. I hope you'll understand and won't be hurt." He halted in the doorway and stared in astonishment.

Margaret sat in the small walnut rocker she used when hand sewing. She rocked slowly back and forth. The window cast the late afternoon light across her face, causing her wet cheeks to glisten. With both hands, she clutched something too small for him to see against her chest. A tear flowed softly down each cheek, dropping onto her clasped hands. She looked up at Dan. Her normally impeccable make-up was smeared. Gently, she lowered her hands to reveal the lifeless body of her parakeet, Petey.

Dan knew the bird held special meaning for Margaret. It was the last gift her husband gave her before he died of a sudden heart attack. Dan had inadvertently discovered that each evening, when she thought no one was listening, Margaret related the day's events to Petey, the way she must have done with her husband.

Dan knelt beside her rocker. "What happened?"

"I was sweeping the carpet in the hallway. The cord caught on the cage stand and, before I realized what was happening, pulled it over. The bottom of the cage broke loose, and Petey escaped." Softly, she smoothed a feather on the stilled wing. "Petey landed on the floor, right in front of Princess's nose. She grabbed him by the neck. Petey squawked once and died. It all happened so fast, there was nothing I could do." The tears flowed faster.

Dan gave her his handkerchief and patted her arm. She wiped her eyes and looked at him. She said, as much to convince herself as him, "My cats know not to bother Petey. But even humans will react instinctively, without thinking, when the conditions are right. Princess realized immediately what she had done. She dropped Petey, made a little cry, and ran into the utility room. She always hides there when she's upset."

Margaret gently stroked Petey's tiny body. "I know Princess didn't mean it. But it hurts *so much* when one that you love harms another you love." Her tears poured. Dan held her against his shoulder and let her cry it out.

An hour later, Margaret watched Dan use a garden trowel to dig a small hole in the flowerbed beside the house. Soggy brown stubble was all that remained of the flowers. Wrapped in a white handkerchief that had belonged to Margaret's husband, Petey lay beside Dan's foot.

A door opened next door. Laurie and her parents hurried over. Catherine said, "We saw you from the kitchen window. What is going on?"

Margaret pulled her husband's old jacket closer around her. Her gray-green eyes filled with tears. "Princess killed Petey."

"What! How?"

As Margaret explained, Dan placed Petey in the grave and covered him up. He gave the tiny mound a final pat, stood up, and brushed the wet dirt from his knees. He glanced around, unsure of what to do next.

Margaret stepped closer to Petey's grave. "I want to say a prayer."

Dan was taken aback. It seemed silly to pray over a bird. But when he saw the Carpenters respectively bow their heads, he followed suit.

In a voice muffled by the wind and her tears, Margaret prayed. "Lord, I know all life is a manifestation of you. That your energy flows equally in the tiny violet and the great redwood, the microscopic amoeba and the mighty elephant, and as well in man."

She knelt and ran her finger lightly over the small grave. "Please take this minute particle of yourself back into your bosom. Let this tiny drop of life's energy flow joyously in the current of your great loving spirit, and be one with you in peace and love. Amen."

She rose and started to turn away. Then halted, and lowered her head again. "There is one more thing, Lord. Please touch my heart and help me to forgive Princess. I've already forgiven her on an intellectual level, but I need your help to forgive her emotionally. Thank you. Amen."

Margaret's prayer touched Dan's heart, in spite of himself. His mind started whirling again over what to do.

Catherine put her arm around Margaret. "Why don't you and Dan come to our house for a cup of tea. It will do you good."

Margaret nodded and allowed herself to be led toward their house. Suddenly, she swung around and looked at Dan. "I almost forgot. Weren't you saying something about needing to talk to me when you came through the door this afternoon?"

Dan glanced sideways at Laurie and reddened. "It isn't important. I figured out the answer myself. It's not worth mentioning now. You go on. I'll be there after I put the garden trowel away." Laurie waited until her parents and Margaret had moved out of earshot. She turned a smiling face to Dan. "You have changed your mind, haven't you? You are staying."

Dan nodded. "Margaret always seemed so invincible, so proper. Like a great lady always under control. Petey's death shook her hard. I didn't realize she could be so vulnerable. She is like a brokenhearted little girl. But I haven't changed my mind about her gift and I trust her even less than I did before. I just couldn't add to her hurt right now. I've gotten along with her so far. It won't hurt to wait a little while longer."

Laurie smiled teasingly. "But you said nothing, *absolutely* nothing, could change your mind."

Dan scowled at her. "Why don't you shut up." He stomped off toward the garage, acutely aware that Laurie continued to watch him with an irritating grin on her face.

CHAPTER SEVEN

Dan had meant it when he told Laurie he would stay, but as his pity for Margaret lessened, his uncertainty about associating with someone possessing an evil power returned. As far as he could tell, living with Margaret had not harmed him yet, and there was no sign it was about to. However, to be on the safe side, he investigated the possibility of getting an apartment of his own. The cost was much higher than he figured. He inquired into the probability of getting scholarships and was told none were available.

During Thanksgiving break, he talked to his home bank about a loan. He was informed that they had quit giving student loans because too many students had defaulted on them. And his ex-friend's illegal use of his identity was still affecting his credit rating. However, since he and his parents were established customers, they might be willing to arrange a personal loan if his parents agreed to cosign. He knew that was impossible because his mother still strongly disapproved of his going to college.

The only option left was to get a full-time job. But he knew he wasn't a strong enough student to handle both work and the class loads he always carried. Things weren't desperate enough yet for him to be willing to lengthen the time needed to get his degree by reducing his class schedule. He reluctantly decided to stay put. However, he kept the option of a full-time job stored at the back of his mind, in case something happened to alter his decision.

One evening, in the middle of December, Dan took the kitchen faucet handle apart to fix a leak. Margaret and Sobra were out on patrol.

After consulting with Sergeant Beacon, she and Sobra walked the neighborhood every evening looking for more traps. Five were found before anything was harmed. A sixth wasn't found in time. An elderly neighbor, too crippled to walk her old fox terrier on a leash, lost her constant companion. The little dog suffered agony before Margaret and Sobra discovered him. He died on the way to the veterinarian. While all the traps were found within a six-block radius of Bill Saxon's home, Margaret failed to find conclusive proof that he had anything to do with them.

A blast of cold air announced Margaret and Sobra's return. Dan glanced up from his work. "You're back early. Everything okay?"

Margaret's upper lip disappeared in a smile. "It couldn't be better." She unleashed Sobra, who headed for her water bowl. Margaret tossed back the hood of her snow-covered coat. "I just received an early Christmas present."

Dan slipped a new washer into place as he asked, "What's that?"

"I spoke to Mrs. Reynolds, the Saxon's neighbor. Bill and one of his friends have left for California. Bill *told* Mrs. Reynolds that they had a job waiting."

"What do you mean, 'Bill *told*'?"

"Bill's mother let it slip to Mrs. Reynolds that the police were questioning some of his friends about the series of robberies that have occurred around town. Mrs. Reynolds figures they arranged to leave town before they got caught."

"Good riddance to a real jerk."

Margaret shot Dan a disapproving look, but waited to speak. She plugged in the coffeemaker and hung her coat in the pantry.

Dan hurried to clean up his mess so he could relax and enjoy a cup of coffee before getting back to his studies. He joined Margaret at the table.

She took a sip, eyeing him over the edge of her cup, trying to decide how to begin. Sitting her cup down, she leaned forward. "I can understand how you feel about Bill. No one is any happier than I am to see him leave town. He has given nothing but heartache to people, and pain and death to animals. But I have also known a different Bill. I can remember a carefree little boy, who played on my front porch and thought I made the greatest oatmeal cookies in the whole world.

"That little boy worshipped his daddy. Unfortunately, his father only saw Bill as a nuisance. Bill knew just how close he could get before his father would slap him, ordering Bill to stay away from him while he worked on his cars or did yard work. There were many times when I saw Bill standing a safe distance away, hands behind his back, happily watching his daddy. Content just to be near him.

"Something shattered in Bill after his father deserted the family. About the time Bill turned ten. From then on he became an increasing discipline problem for his male teachers. He dropped out of school as soon as he turned sixteen. He has grown into a vindictive young man, who can't hold what few jobs he's qualified for because of his habit of getting into fights and not wanting to take orders. No employment has led him into stealing to get money. I wouldn't be surprised if he isn't also into drugs."

"Why does he hate animals so much?"

"Bill's father took his two hunting dogs with him when he left. Can you imagine how it must have hurt little Bill to realize that the father he had worshipped prized his animals more than him? He has been taking his repressed anger out on all animals ever since."

"I see." Dan took a sip of coffee as he pondered her information. "It's too bad someone didn't help Bill."

"I tried. Others have tried. He was offered psychotherapy. But no one can help a person who refuses to see that he is the one with the emotional problem. According to Bill, it's always everybody else's fault when something goes wrong. Until he wakes up and sees the truth, the only thing anyone can do is to keep him from inflicting his pain on others as much as possible."

"I'm still glad to be rid of him."

"So am I. But I wanted you to know a little more about Bill. I don't want you thinking he is a complete monster. I still harbor the hope that something will happen one day to wake him up. Everyone has the capacity for manifesting either a Christ-like light generated by love or darkness generated by fear and ignorance. Regardless of which appears to predominate, always remember the other is present in them somewhere. The right situations could help it emerge."

Dan thought of Margaret's gift—the good she seemed to do with it and the evil he was now convinced it was based on. He chuckled nervously. "I'll try to keep that in mind."

Margaret gave him a puzzled look, waiting for him to elaborate on his response. When he didn't, she said, "Bill's leaving isn't the only cheerful news I've heard." She took a sip of coffee. "I stopped in to see Mrs. Campbell."

"Who?"

"The elderly neighbor who lost her dog in the trap Bill set. The shelter for homeless animals has been trying to find a home for a small mixed-breed dog. The dog is seven years old, housebroken, and spayed. She had belonged to an elderly gentleman who died recently. Mrs. Campbell has tentatively agreed to take her. The poor woman is still fearful of losing another pet."

"That's interesting. I didn't know her name, but I've been thinking about her myself. I've studied her backyard as I passed it on my way back and forth to campus. Someone could string a heavy wire from her back door, across the yard, to that post near her garage. Then he could fasten an extra long chain to the wire and put a nail near the back door to hang the loose end on when it's not in use. All Mrs. Campbell would have to do is open the door and hook the chain to the dog's collar. Since her yard has no trees or bushes to get tangled around, the dog would have the whole area to exercise in. And Mrs. Campbell wouldn't have to worry about it leaving her property and getting hurt."

Margaret smiled. "That is a wonderful idea. How nice of you to think of it. I'll provide the wire and chain if you'll do the work."

Uncomfortable with her praise, Dan squirmed and quickly added, "I'm going home next week for Christmas break. So I'll have to do it this Saturday. Is that okay?"

"It's perfect. I promised to deliver the dog that afternoon." She leaned back in her chair. "I can't remember when I've felt so good. Giving an old woman a bit of happiness while helping a homeless animal find a new life is a tremendous lift to the spirits." She smiled at Dan, who was putting his cup in the dishwasher. "You've made it even better by coming up with the idea that will alleviate Mrs. Campbell's worst fears. She'll be thanking you all over the place."

Dan blushed. He didn't want any thanks. But he knew how Margaret felt. Laurie was keeping a parakeet for him at her house. A girl in his computer class couldn't keep the bird, and hadn't been able to find someone to take it. Naïve enough to believe it could fend for itself in the middle of December, she was planning to turn it loose, when Dan overheard her tell a classmate about it. Laurie was to give it to Margaret after he left for Christmas break.

He gave her strict instructions to tell Margaret all about the bird, except his part in it. He did not want Margaret to know he had rescued it for her. She could misconstrue his gesture. He was more determined than ever to keep their relationship on a business-only level.

Margaret picked up the forgiven Princess and stroked her. Dan smiled. Yes, he knew exactly how she felt about Mrs. Campbell and the dog. The phone rang. Margaret put Princess down and headed for the hallway. Dan could hear her talking as he switched off the kitchen light. "How long has your dog been misbehaving?"

Dan's mood vanished. Annoyed, he marched past her, heading upstairs to his room. As always, just when he was feeling relaxed around Margaret, something happened to remind him to keep his guard up. However, he wasn't going to think about it now. He needed to finish the report for his principles of management course, which was due before the holiday break.

As it had been with every school vacation, Christmas break was a strain for Dan. He had to watch his every word to make sure he didn't let anything slip about Margaret. And his mother added to his nervousness by studying him like a cat watching a bird, ready to pounce if she detected any change in him that would endanger his immortal soul. Though he hated to admit it to himself, it was a relief to get back to Margaret's.

January found Margaret busy training her new bird, Corky. Dan and Laurie were adjusting to new schedules that always came with the change of semesters. The weather was unseasonably mild and appreciated by Dan and Laurie as they walked to school, remembering the bitter cold of the previous winter.

While the winter was warmer, Dan's feelings for Laurie were cooler. His increased distrust of Margaret had spilled over into their relationship. If Margaret had an evil power, how had it affected Laurie who was always ready to defend her? Until he knew for sure, he was keeping it friendly but cool. He repressed his deepening desire for her, denying to himself that it even existed.

Perturbed and hurt by his standoffishness since Petey's burial, Laurie had tried to draw the reason out of him. He retreated further into his shell. She tried to tease him out of his mood and failed. She gave up, hoping that time would take care of whatever the problem was.

One evening in late January Dan and Margaret joined a large assortment of Carpenter friends and relatives in their living room. It was Frank Carpenter's fifty-fifth birthday. He stood beside a card table piled high with gifts. Each unwrapping brought forth oh's and ah's from the crowd. Dan and the two Carpenter sisters watched from folding chairs lined up against the wall and next to the door that led to the kitchen.

Sharon leaned across Dan to confide to Laurie. "We'll have some cute gifts when we get home. Lady was starting into labor when we left."

Laurie stared at her in astonishment. "I thought she wasn't due for three more days."

Sharon shrugged. "She decided to come early."

"And you left her alone after Margaret warned you that her condition was too poor for another litter?"

Sharon reddened. "Tom wouldn't have it any other way. He said animal birthing is such a natural process that it doesn't need to be supervised. Besides, he enjoys parties and didn't want to miss this one."

Laurie forced her anger-filled voice to stay low. "A birthday party is more important than a life? More important than preventing needless suffering?"

"Lady's got a bigger whelping box this time. She is also more experienced. What happened before can't happen again. Tom insisted that nothing else could go wrong."

"Tom is an ignoramus. He doesn't know better. But you, Sharon. What's your excuse? You know some animals can have as much of a problem giving birth as some women do. How could you leave Lady like that?"

Sharon crossed her arms in a huff, and stared straight ahead without answering. Laurie sat tight-lipped.

Dan suddenly felt trapped in the center of a cold war. He figured a closed mouth was the safest course. Besides, he could understand both girls' points of view. Since his own family had also given the needs of their pets the very lowest priority, he wasn't sure who was right. He tried to concentrate on the gift openings.

Laurie motioned to Margaret, who sat in the far corner with Laurie's cat curled up in her lap. Margaret put the cat down, weaved her way through the guests and squatted next to Laurie. "What's wrong?"

"Sharon here said that Lady is in labor right now."

Margaret gave a start and looked at Sharon. "Starting into labor three days early could mean trouble. Don't you think you had better go home and check on her?"

Sharon shook her head. "Tom wouldn't like it."

"Do it anyway."

"I can't!"

Everyone in the room stared at them. Catherine shot her daughters a look of warning. Margaret whispered, "Let's go into the kitchen." A curious Dan tagged along.

As soon as the door was closed, Laurie turned to Sharon. "You have to check on Lady. You'll never forgive yourself if you don't and something happens."

The door opened and Tom peeked in. "What's going on?"

Margaret said, "We are trying to convince Sharon to go check on Lady."

Tom closed the door behind him. "Why?"

"She could be in trouble."

Tom's redhead complexion got redder. "You don't know that. You're just guessing. We are not going to get into trouble with my in-laws on your say-so." He put his arm possessively around Sharon. "Come on honey. Let's go back inside before people start wondering."

Sharon looked pleadingly at him. "Maybe we should check. Lady has acted funny the last couple of days."

"No. Now move."

Dan watched them leave, then asked Laurie, "Is Tom right? Would your parents have been upset if they had stayed home to keep an eye on Lady?"

"Of course not. Dad would've been disappointed they couldn't make it to his party. But he would have understood. It's Tom who can't understand. If it were his father's birthday, his family would be furious if he had stayed home for a mere dog. Tom won't see that Dad doesn't think the same way as his parents."

Margaret sighed. "Well, there is nothing we can do about it now. We might as well rejoin the party."

Everyone returned to his or her original positions. Except Tom. He sat at Sharon's feet and flashed Dan and Laurie a look of disgust as they sat down. The four turned their attention to Frank. He unwrapped a package and held up a blue dress shirt for all to admire.

Laurie nudged Dan. "Margaret is doing her thing."

Dan glanced at Margaret. She had shifted her folding chair as far into the corner, and away from distractions, as she could get. She sat with feet flat on the floor, eyes closed, and palms up in her lap. Suddenly her eyes flew open. She jumped up and hurriedly made her way through the guests.

With a no-nonsense, monarchical expression, she addressed Tom and Sharon in a low voice. "Look you two. I just tried to contact Lady. Something *is* wrong. It may already be too late. Now either one or both of you come with me to unlock your door, or I'm going over there by myself and break in. It doesn't matter to me, which it is, as long as Lady gets the help she needs. Now, what's it going to be?"

The couple glanced at each other. Sharon looked relieved. Tom frowned disapprovingly at her, then turned to Margaret. "I'll go. But if this is a wild goose chase, I'll never let you forget it." He grabbed Sharon's hand. "You come with us. I want you to see once and for all how crazy Margaret really is. Then maybe you'll quit nagging me to listen to her."

Laurie spoke up. "Dan and I are going too." She stood up. "I'll explain the situation to Mom while you get our coats."

Margaret pushed past Tom as soon as he opened his door. Without waiting for a light, she hurriedly stumbled through the dim house to the basement. The others followed as Tom turned on the lights.

They found her kneeling beside Lady. The Labrador retriever laid on her side in the whelping box. A dead pup hung half-in, half-out of her vagina. A sorrowful Margaret looked at Laurie. "We're too late."

The two couples gathered around the front of the whelping box. They stood in silence. All eyes were riveted on Lady's lifeless form, willing her to move, to prove there was still life. Nothing happened.

Tears drifted down Sharon's cheeks. Margaret rose and put an arm around her. "Let's go upstairs. There is nothing we can do here."

Sharon looked Margaret squarely in the face. "You must hate us."

Margaret shook her head sadly. "I can't afford it. If I hated everyone who mistreated animals, I'd be a bitter, worn-down, spiritless old woman. I refuse to become an additional victim of cruelty by filling myself with hatred for the cruel and ignorant." She maneuvered Sharon toward the stairs. "Why don't we go upstairs and make some hot tea. I think everyone could use a cup."

Laurie followed them. Dan hesitated, waiting for Tom. Tom's attention was still focused on Lady. He sank to his knees beside her and gently stroked her head. "I'm sorry, Lady. I'm sorry." He grabbed up her lifeless body. Clutching her to his chest, he rocked back and forth. "I'm sorry. So sorry." The stocky-built mechanic wept over his dog. Dan slipped quietly upstairs, leaving him alone.

He joined Laurie and Margaret, sitting at the kitchen table. Sharon stood by the stove waiting for the water to boil. In a determined tone they'd never heard before, she said, "I promise you, all of you, that I will never allow another animal to suffer needlessly because I lacked the gumption to take responsibility when it was needed." The three nodded in agreement. A new fire burned in Sharon. They sensed she would keep her word.

CHAPTER EIGHT

Spring arrived. The evening was warm and humid. A light breeze stirred Dan's bedroom curtains. He sat hunched over his desk, trying unsuccessfully to study for a test. Earlier in the evening, a phone call requesting Margaret's services had started his mind whirling again. Since the last episode with Lady, he had found it increasingly difficult to keep his thoughts off her gift and on his schoolwork.

Margaret's being right *again* had finally started to create tiny cracks in the certainty of his beliefs. The questions had haunted him. They were quiet while he worked with his hands around the house. But the minute he turned to the mental work of his studies, they clamored for answers.

Could everything his mother's church had preached about psychic powers being from the devil be wrong? But if Margaret's gift was of God, why didn't it work perfectly all the time? Why hadn't she foreseen Lady's trouble in time to save her? Was Laurie right? That

ESP was neither good nor evil, but could be used for either. It was just a natural ability that, like most skills and talents, sometimes worked better at one time than another for the possessor. And there were differing types and levels of ability among those so talented.

The thought that it was natural disturbed him far more than did the idea that evil was at the root of Margaret's gift. A black and white world of good and evil was easier to deal with. It made it more clear cut as to who was responsible for positive and negative happenings. If Laurie was right, then there was more to the mental-spiritual capabilities of man and animal than he cared to admit. And probably more mental-spiritual responsibility and control by the average man and woman over his or her own life situations than most realized. Was Laurie right? For days, weeks, months, the questions tormented him, making it more difficult for him to keep up his grades.

He, unknowingly, tapped his pen against his papers, tempting Taylor to leave his towel and bat at the jiggling pen. Dan smiled at him. He stroked the purring cat, while he tried to figure a way to gain some peace of mind. What he needed, he decided, was more information. He could ask Laurie, but he would only be getting her opinion. He could do some research on the subject, but that would take more time than he could spare. Besides, he might get into some dark areas he didn't want to deal with. He knew only one quick authoritative source.

If he asked Margaret directly about the story behind her gift, he might get a clue giving him an answer he could accept, within the context of what he already believed. But he didn't relish the idea of questioning her. Fear clung to the edge of his thoughts. He might not be able to handle what she would say. Instead of helping, it could confuse matters even more. And, besides, evil was nothing to fool around with.

No, he decided, it was better to live with the unanswered questions, than to risk delving into something that could be dangerous. The tiny cracks that had begun to form in his mind were sealed up. He picked up his class notes and forced himself to concentrate on his studying. But it wasn't easy.

One hot August Saturday, Dan stood on a stepladder painting Margaret's garage. He had followed the shade as long as possible. Now he worked on the alley side, sweating as he painted under the baking sun.

"Hello, college boy."

Dan glanced down and nearly dropped his paintbrush. Bill Saxon stood in the middle of the alley, squinting up at him. The big man wore an obnoxious grin. Dan had stayed up too late the night before, working on a class report. He was hot, tired, sweaty, and in no mood for the likes of Bill.

Forcing himself to remain composed, Dan wiped his brow with the back of his hand, dipped his brush in the bucket of white paint, and spread it on the overhang. As politely as he could muster, he said, "I thought you were in California."

In a tone filled with disappointment, Bill said, "Got back five days ago." He looked as if he wanted to punch someone. "Things didn't work out like I planned."

He surveyed Margaret's backyard. "Where's that dumb dog?"

Dan scowled. Sobra wasn't dumb. Besides, he wasn't about to tell a thief like Bill Saxon that Margaret's watchdog wasn't home. Margaret had been invited to spend a few days at a friend's cabin on the lake. She'd asked permission to take Sobra along so she could introduce her to new experiences. Dan answered, "She's around."

Bill sneered. "She better not bark at me."

Dan spoke without thinking. "Why? Aren't you man enough to take it?"

One glimpse of Bill's expression told Dan he had said the wrong thing. Bill clenched his fists. He moved towards Dan, clearly intending to jerk Dan off the ladder and beat him into the ground.

Dan broke out in a solid sweat that had nothing to do with the August heat. He saw Bill coming as if in slow motion. He was even conscious of a sweat bee buzzing around his own forehead. He tried to swallow the lump in his throat. He was no fistfighter. He didn't stand a chance against the bigger more experienced Bill. He had to think of something quick.

As Bill grabbed his leg, Dan seized the half-full paint bucket and dumped it on Bill's head.

Bill flopped around like an ostrich trying to fly. He sent the paint bucket skipping and banging down the alley. He shouted, "I'm going to kill you!" White paint ran into his mouth. He spit it out. "I'm going to kill you!"

Dan stood paralyzed on the ladder, wondering what it felt like to die.

Bill wiped away paint threatening to run into his eyes. He spit out more paint. He sputtered, "I'm going to kill you!" A stream of paint rolled down and into his nose. Between violent snorts, he yelled, "I'm going to kill you!"

Suddenly, a deep male voice said, "No you're not."

Dan turned to see two men walking up beside his ladder. One, an African-American man who looked like a prizefighter, was wearing a city policeman's uniform. He was so large that comparing him to Bill was like comparing an elephant to a draft horse. The officer pointed his thick thumb at Dan while addressing Bill. "If I hear that one hair on this man's head has been harmed, I'm coming after you. Do you hear me?"

Bill had stopped his flopping. He hung his dripping head. "Yes."

"Yes, what?"

"Yes, Sergeant Beacon."

"That's better." The sergeant eyed the starchless Bill. "While we're on the subject of your forthcoming good behavior, let me warn you. If I hear of one animal being hurt or killed in this neighborhood, I am going to investigate it personally. Do you understand me?"

"Yes. Sergeant Beacon."

"Good. I like it when we understand each other so well." He held up his big, dark hands and flexed his fingers. "It saves on my knuckles." He motioned towards the small white man, wearing a business suit, who accompanied him. "This is Police Lieutenant Webster. He has come all the way from California to ask you some questions about a murder connected to a series of robberies that took place out there."

Alarm fluttered across Bill's features—what could be seen of them. He looked down at himself. "I need to get cleaned up."

Sergeant Beacon flashed him a big, congenial smile. "Of course you do. You just go and get washed up. Take your time. We'll just visit with your mother while we wait. She's such a pleasant woman. I never saw a mother who liked to talk so much about her son."

Bill reddened between the streaks of white paint. He headed for home, flanked on each side by a police officer.

Trembling from relief, Dan eased himself down the ladder. When he reached the ground, he grabbed the ladder for support. His legs felt as stiff as rubber bands. As he stood regaining strength, he realized he still clutched his paintbrush. He muttered to himself, "Looks like I need to get another bucket of paint." He dropped the brush in a can of water to keep it from drying out. "But first, I think I'd better go to the bathroom." He headed for the house, questioning his own manhood because he had felt afraid and because he couldn't beat Bill in a straight fight.

Margaret arrived home from her trip the next day. Later that same evening, she and Laurie were relaxing in Margaret's porch swing. Dan was perched on the edge of the porch, his back against the railing. They all sipped ice tea, enjoying the summer breeze. A lingering whiff of a neighbor's barbecue drifted across to them.

Princess was curled up in Margaret's lap, and Sobra lay at her feet. Taylor was inside, watching them from an open window. Katy rubbed against Dan's legs. He took a drink of tea, then reached down and scratched her head. Dan had just finished telling the women about the episode with Bill. All three emitted an occasional chuckle at the lingering image of Bill dripping with white paint.

Suddenly, Laurie frowned. "Dan, do you realize Bill could have beaten you badly? Even killed you?"

"I know," he answered worriedly. "And he still might try."

Margaret smiled. "I don't think so."

Laurie and Dan spoke in unison. "Why not?"

"Because of Sergeant Beacon's reputation."

Dan snapped his fingers. "Now I remember. I thought there was something familiar about his name. Beacon is the policeman you consulted after Katy was hurt. The one you said helps at the shelter."

"That's right. He and his wife are two of our best supporters. She grew up here and has been involved since she was a teenager."

Laurie asked impatiently, "What about his reputation?"

"He is an ex-boxer, ex-marine, and grew up in the slums of New York City. With that type of background, plus his size, it is easy for him to intimidate small-town thugs like Bill. It's rumored he was fired from his job in New York for losing his temper and nearly beating a thug to death." She took a sip of tea. "I don't believe it. From offhand remarks he's made, I'm convinced the sergeant started the rumor himself to put the fear of Beacon into the local criminal element. To the best of my knowledge, he's never laid a hand on anyone. He's made sure he doesn't have too."

Dan said, "Well, he definitely had Bill cringing."

"That's why you don't have anything to worry about. Bill's not going to risk crossing him."

Dan lifted his glass in salute. "Here's to Sergeant Beacon. May he stay healthy and live long—at least until I finish school and leave town."

The two women chuckled. Laurie turned to Margaret. "Then we won't have to worry about Bill bothering our pets either?"

"Not as long a he's afraid of Beacon."

The evening's conversation had made Dan feel more at ease with Margaret than normal. And the mention of animals brought all his questions to mind. Though several months had passed, the unanswered questions still gave him frequent trouble when he tried to concentrate on his schoolwork. He didn't want to explore them, but the constant mental battle to push them away had worn him down. Now was the time to try to put some of them to rest, he reluctantly concluded.

He sat his glass on the porch floor, picked up a purring Katy, and stroked her soft fur. "Speaking of animals, Margaret. When did you first realize you had a special gift?"

Margaret was startled. She scrutinized him, trying to determine his sudden interest after all this time. After what seemed an uncomfortably long time to Dan, she smiled. She leaned back in the swing. Rocking gently, she said, "I have always felt an affinity with nature. I must have either been born with my gift or possessed it from a very early age. Only, it was so natural for me, I wasn't fully aware of it. Not until the episode with the rats."

Laurie shivered. "Rats?"

Margaret chuckled at Laurie's reaction. "That's right. I was twelve at the time. My parents owned a hundred-acre farm in Northern Indiana. A common problem for farmers is when a colony of rats build nests under their chicken houses. Rats can destroy eggs, baby chicks, and feed. That summer Mr. Peterson, our closest neighbor, had a heavy infestation of them. The biggest problem was how to get rid of the rats without harming the chickens. Poisons wouldn't work in that situation.

"Mr. Peterson consulted my father. After much deliberation they came up with a plan. First, they would use old rags to stuff the openings of all the rat holes they could find. Then they would run a hose from my father's portable gasoline engine to a rat hole and fill the rats' caverns with carbon monoxide.

"School was out, and I was bored. Always curious concerning anything to do with animals, I begged to be allowed to watch. They relented only after I swore I wouldn't get in the way."

She remembered stepping into the hot, stuffy chicken house and wrinkling her nose. The usual odors of chicken feathers, feed, and straw were extra heavy because Mr. Peterson did not clean as often as he should have. A thick layer of chicken manure coated everything. She gingerly stepped over to the roost where she could watch the men stuffing the holes, while staying out of the way. Most of the chickens were outdoors where it was cooler. Her father started his loud, clanking engine. The few remaining chickens abandoned their nests with a flurry.

Her father and Mr. Peterson held pitchforks, poised to stab any rat that tried to escape. They underestimated the number of rat holes. Several rats bolted from hidden openings, scurried frantically around the room, and out the door. The men tried desperately to fork them. The rats were faster.

Young Margaret watched in fascination, until, suddenly, a feeling of terror overwhelmed her. Outwardly, she was fine. But inwardly, she felt as if she were choking and gasping for breath. It was a strange feeling. On one level she was calm. On another, she was agitated, frightened, suffocating. The sense of panic grew until she could not take it. Just as Mr. Peterson impaled a squealing rat on a pitchfork prong, she bolted out the door along with the rodents and ran the mile and half to their farm.

Her father found her shivering in her room. "I'm sorry, kitten. I shouldn't have let you go with me. It was too much for a young girl to watch."

Margaret knew there was more to it than that. She had never been the queasy type. It took her quite a while to figure it out. Then one day, as she was feeding their chickens, it dawned on her. Though she had never heard of psychic ability at that time, she realized she had somehow tuned into those rats. She had felt the panic, choking, and dying of the rats trapped in their tunnels. The same terror from choking that compelled the luckier ones to escape had forced her to run.

She could not help it. Though she knew that the rats had to be killed, she leaned against the chicken house and wept because of the suffering they had endured.

After that, she began to experiment with the animals on their farm. With practice, she found she could usually sense what they were feeling. She was more successful with some animals than others. She was best with cats and dogs, because she felt the greatest affinity with them.

About a year after the incident at Mr. Peterson's, one of her father's heifers was ailing. Margaret told him exactly what the cow was feeling. After he got over the shock of discovering she was right, he took advantage of her gift. Whenever he had a problem with an animal, he would have her see if she could help determine the cause. That was the beginning of her using her gift to help people understand their animals.

A cloudbank had darkened the evening sky as Margaret finished her story. Silence prevailed while the three people sank into their own thought worlds. Sobra and the cats slept. The summer breeze carried the sounds of a neighborhood settling in for the night. Laurie rattled the ice in her glass. She lifted it, trying to shake out the last drop of tea.

A mosquito buzzed Dan's ear. He swatted at it and missed. He waited until it landed on his cheek, then smacked it. He glanced up in triumph at the two women. A light from the living room window revealed Margaret's face. She was watching him.

With a start, Dan realized she was waiting for his reaction to her story. He had to say something. But what? The truth? That he had immediately dismissed her account as nothing more than an excitable, pubertal girl reacting to a stifling chicken house and disgusting rats. That it hadn't proved a thing except that Margaret had a lively imagination as a child. That he did not believe rats were capable of feeling what she claimed. No. He couldn't tell her that. He didn't want to risk upsetting her. He was still too dependent on her for room and board.

He tapped his glass, knocking an ice cube into his mouth. He sucked on it as he tried to figure out what to say. Then he remembered there was something that did not match up with his own observations. If he threw her more questions, maybe it would keep him from having to express his own opinions. He dropped the ice cube back into his glass. "Margaret, there is something I don't understand."

"What is it?"

"According to your rat story and what you've told me before, you experience only what the animals feel. But when Katy was in trouble, you said you just sensed it without the information coming from her. How could you have done that?"

Margaret smiled. "You're partly right, Dan. I do get a visual image of what the animal sees. That's how I could describe the settings. For many years, what the animal actually saw or felt was all I ever had to go on. Then an incident happened that increased my powers of perception."

Margaret thought for a couple of minutes. She frowned. "I don't think I can explain it adequately. It was such a profound, mystical experience. A fleeting, unexpected tuning into the universe. I was thirty-five, a housewife, and at peace with the world and myself.

"One spring day, I was hanging sheets on the line. In a split-second, I found myself in a state of enlightenment. I believe metaphysicians call it cosmic consciousness." She hesitated, struggling for words.

"For a flash, an instant, I understood the meaning of the universe. The nature of God. Of man. Though I had already vaguely sensed it through the animals, I *experienced* all life as one. I don't just believe it. I *know* eternal life exists in all matter, whether it be rock or man."

Taken aback, Dan nearly dropped his glass. "Are you claiming you had a religious experience similar to what saints and holy men supposedly have?"

"It's probably on the same order, yes."

Laurie asked, "How did that broaden your ability with animals?"

"I sensed on a deeper level the universal intelligence, the guiding influence, operating in the world. After that cosmic experience of oneness, I started experimenting with ways to tune into that intelligence for aid and communion. That is when I began using relaxation, or meditative, exercises in my consultations. Sometimes it helps. Often, I still only experience what the animal experiences, as I always did. But there are other times when my spirit, the animal's spirit, and God's Holy Spirit—or Universal Mind, if you prefer—are at one. Such times enable me to gain deeper insights into the situation than I ordinarily would. And it seems to work only when the additional insight is acutely needed to solve the problem."

Dan had heard all he could stand. He leaped to his feet. "It's getting late. I have studying to do. I'll see you both in the morning." He rushed into the house before the women could respond.

He hurried to his room, with Taylor trailing. His mind whirled angrily. Now, on top of everything else, Margaret maintains she's had a mystical encounter as well. He was shocked to the core by her heresy. Margaret was no saint. Common, ordinary people like her and him just didn't have such experiences. Margaret either made up the whole thing or she had suffered a hallucination. The only way he would ever be convinced that such an experience could really happen to someone like her was if he had such an experience himself. And that was impossible.

CHAPTER NINE

Early autumn was unseasonably cold and wet. Continual wind and rain had forced the leaves down prematurely, creating a soggy, brown cover in places. One morning Dan and Laurie were forced to walk around or through the leaf piles, on their way to campus. The trees still dripped from an earlier, brief squall. The sky declared another storm was approaching.

Dan was unmindful of the need to hurry before the next rainstorm arrived. He strolled alone, whistling a cheerful tune. Laurie plodded, downcast, beside him. A drop of water from an overhead branch struck her forehead, startling her. Dan chuckled at her sour expression as she wiped her face.

Annoyed, she asked, "Doesn't this weather get you down?"

"I'm in too good a mood to let a little wetness bother me."

"You've been as cheerful as a little boy on the first day of summer vacation ever since this semester started. Why?"

"I'm now officially a senior." He shifted his books and waved his freed arm happily, joyously. "The end of school is finally in sight. My dream of a business career is finally going to become a reality in just a few more months." He didn't add so was his dream of moving out of Margaret's life. Puzzled by Laurie's frown, he asked, "Why have you been so grumpy since school started? You're graduating this coming spring too."

"I've enjoyed my college years. I'm not as anxious as you are to see them end."

"Doesn't Indiana require its teachers to take continuing education courses? You'll need more college for that."

"Yes, but it won't be the same."

"Why not?"

Laurie glared at him as if he had turned dimwitted. "For one thing I'll be working full-time and taking classes only part-time. For another thing." She motioned from her to him and back again. "It won't be like this."

Baffled, Dan asked, "Like what?"

"You know. Us."

"Us?"

Laurie eyed him sadly and sighed. "We won't be together anymore. We'll be in different towns. Maybe even different states." Tears filled her eyes. "After graduation we may never ever see each other again."

"Oh." Dan's happy mood vanished. He thought for a second, then said, "We still have till spring."

"Not really. I'm going to be student teaching next semester at the high school across town. I'll be catching a ride everyday." Wondering to herself why he had let it be so, she added, "Our walks to and from campus have been our only real times alone together. And they will stop at the end of this semester."

"Oh." Dan's shoulders drooped. He and Laurie walked the rest of the way in silence. Neither paid any attention to the light drizzle that started as they separated for their classes.

Dan spent the rest of the day in a daze. Laurie had jolted him into facing a reality he had not seriously considered—the end of their relationship. Suddenly all the longings for her that he had managed to repress for nearly two and half years burst forth, threatening to overwhelm him. He tried to force them back, so he could think clearly. He must be realistic, he told himself. No matter how much he desired Laurie, she had still been deeply influenced by Margaret's confusing, but evil, gift. He needed to think this through carefully.

All through October and November he watched Laurie. Studied her. He searched his own mind and heart. How did he really feel about her? He was surprised to discover she had become his best friend. When did that happen? He'd been too focused on getting through school to notice.

But did he love her enough for marriage? He had always been acutely aware she possessed a certain dimply charm that he found alluring. Was what he felt mere physical attraction or something deeper? If it was love, did they have enough in common to make a good marriage? There were definite differences in their outlooks on life. Could they be blended into a satisfying relationship? He knew it was possible, because his own parents had successfully done it. And what about his mother? How would she react to Laurie?

Dan felt he was on an emotional seesaw. Laurie would express some outrageous belief reminiscent of Margaret, and he would make up his mind. There was no way they could have a good marriage. Then Laurie would say or do something so appealing his resolve melted. How could he ever be happy without her bright, energetic spirit beside him?

In early December he made his decision. For the first time since he had started college, he took a weekend off. He hitched a ride with another homebound student.

He returned late Sunday evening. Sobra and the cats were the only ones to greet him. There was a note on the table from Margaret. She had been called out on a consultation. Leftovers were in the refrigerator if he was hungry.

Dan was too excited to eat. He tossed his suitcase into his room and phoned Laurie. "Can you come over? I know it's late. Margaret is out and I want to talk to you where we can be alone. Yes, it's important. You can finish your sewing project tomorrow. Good. Come to the back door. I'll see you in a couple of minutes. Please hurry. Margaret could be back anytime."

He carefully positioned a small box in the middle of the kitchen table. Then he paced the floor until

Laurie knocked at the back door. Before she could get through the door, he pointed at the table and asked, "Is that all right with you?"

She threw back the hood of her coat. "Is what all right?"

He shook his finger at the table. "That."

She glanced at the table and did a double take. Her eyes widened. She stepped slowly forward and gingerly opened the battered ring box. She stood, stunned, staring at the solitary diamond set in an old-fashioned, gold mounting.

Dan shifted around Laurie like a little dog waiting for a treat. "It was my great-grandmother's engagement ring. She willed it to my mother. Mom said she'd let the first son to get married have it."

Laurie barely managed to whisper, "Married."

Dan grinned. "That's right."

Her eyes shifted from the ring to him. "You're really asking me to marry you?"

Dan frowned, confused. "Sure." Suddenly the light went out of his eyes. "Oh, Laurie. I'm sorry. I took it for granted you would want to marry me. It never occurred to me that you might say no." He dropped into a kitchen chair. "All I thought about was getting you the ring before Christmas. I wanted to be sure there was enough time to have it sized for your finger. Then you would have it to wear over the holidays." He slapped his forehead. "How could I have been so stupid?"

Laurie squatted down beside his chair. "Of course I'll marry you, silly. You just took me by surprise.

That's all." She slipped the ring on her finger. "Look, it fits perfectly. Like it was made for me."

Dan stared at her, yielding at last to the longing he had harbored for her. His long repressed desires bubbled to the surface. He pulled her to him. "I love you, Laurie. I just didn't want to admit it to myself until I realized I could lose you."

"Oh, Dan. I've known you were the one for me since the first time I saw you—scruffy, paint-stained clothes and all—standing on Margaret's ladder."

Their first kiss held all the kisses they had denied themselves for nearly two and half years. Slowly, reluctantly, they separated. Dan gave her a peck on her round nose.

Her finger tenderly traced his ear. "There's just one thing, Dan."

"What's that?"

"Now that we're engaged. Don't you think it is time you asked me out on a date?"

Before he could reply, the back door flew open. A surprised Margaret stood, letting in the cold air. Laurie leaped up and ran to her. "Look what Dan just gave me. We're engaged."

Margaret's upper lip disappeared into her smile, the deepest Dan had ever seen it. She shut the door. "It's about time that boy woke up and realized what he had going for him." She hugged Laurie, then Dan. "This calls for a toast. I've got some champagne around here somewhere. It's been waiting a long time for such an occasion." She disappeared into the pantry where they could hear her rummaging around.

Dan spoke loud enough for her to hear. "Margaret, can I ask a favor of you?"

She reappeared, holding up a bottle. "It's not cold, but it will do. What is it, Dan?"

"I would like to borrow your car." He grinned and motioned toward Laurie. "I want to take my to-be wife out on a gen-u-wine date."

Margaret chuckled. "Well, now. If she's foolish enough to trust you with her future happiness, I guess I should be willing to trust you with my car." She handed Dan the bottle. "You pop the cork while I get the glasses."

Dan poured. Margaret lifted her glass. "Here's to your future together. May it always be as bright as it is now." They drank. Suddenly, Margaret looked thoughtful. She sank into a chair.

Laurie put her glass down. "Are you all right, Margaret?"

"I'm fine. I just realized I need to get a wedding gift."

Dan laughed. "You've got plenty of time to think about that. We're not getting married until we've both graduated and at least one of us has a job."

Laurie knelt beside her. "That's right. Besides, you don't have to give us anything. Just coming to our wedding will be all the gift we want."

Margaret patted Laurie's hand. "I know. But I want to get you something." She wrinkled her forehead in thought. "It has to be extra special. Something that reflects the depth of my love for you both. You're like a son and daughter to me." Laurie hugged her.

Dan shifted nervously. There's that like a son bit again. Why did she feel that way? He certainly hadn't done anything to encourage it. Laurie smiled up at him. He immediately forgot Margaret. He grinned. "Laurie, don't you think we had better go tell your parents."

"Oh, yes." She bounced up, grabbed his hand, and started dragging him to the door. "Let's hurry. They may be getting ready for bed."

Dan glanced back at Margaret. "Leave a light on. This could take awhile."

When he returned, Margaret was sitting where they had left her, having a cup of tea and still pondering what to get them.

Dan arranged for Laurie and her parents to visit his family during Christmas break. Before he left for home, he decided to have a heart to heart talk with Laurie. Margaret discreetly left them alone in the living room. They sat down on the sofa.

He explained his mother's strict religious beliefs to Laurie. "For the sake of peace, would you please not share your ideas on religion nor mention Margaret's gift when you meet my parents? And would you please warn your parents so they won't bring up any awkward subjects?"

She kissed him on the cheek. "Of course."

He swallowed. "There is one other thing." He told her of his vow not to let anything change him and of his concerns about her beliefs. "I almost didn't ask you to marry me because I not only can't accept your ideas, I think they are dangerously wrong." He sighed.

"But I just couldn't deny to myself any longer that I love you. I don't want to live without you, in spite of heretical ideas."

She smiled. "Dan, no one has the right to tell another how they should believe. Not even spouses. I'll promise to respect your beliefs, if you'll do the same for mine. When a problem comes up because of them, we'll figure out a compromise."

A relieved Dan held her tight, marveling at how lucky he was.

She added, "I do think you need to be honest with your mother before I meet her. Without going into specifics, just let her know that I don't believe the way she does. If that worries her, tell her she's welcome to pray for me, but to please refrain from personally trying to change me. If she's like you say she is, she'll accept that type of compromise. After all, you said she and your father have been doing that to some degree all their married life."

Dan took her advice. To his surprise, his mother was responsive. For the sake of her relationship with Dan, she was eager to get along with her future daughter-in-law and her family. For the first time since he could remember, she didn't bring up religious issues with her visitors. All had a restrained, but pleasant, time.

It seemed to Dan that December jumped into February while he wasn't looking. Besides his usual class load, he had been immersed in one last major project for Margaret. He had refinished a walnut dining table and matching buffet that had belonged to her grandparents. He was now working on the six matching chairs.

It was nearing midnight. Margaret had retired earlier with a heavy cold. The house was dark except for the basement where Dan worked. He lightly stained a chair sitting on the workbench. Laurie sat on the edge of the bench, lazily swinging her feet. Since their engagement, she often studied, graded papers, or made out lesson plans for her student teaching classes at Margaret's, while Dan worked nearby. But tonight, she had decided to take a much-needed break.

Dan placed the newly stained chair beside the four others waiting for their first coat of varnish. He picked up the last stripped chair, blew Laurie a kiss, and sat the chair on the workbench. He ran his fingers carefully over the sanded wood, feeling for rough spots. He sanded a small spot on the seat. Engrossed in his work, he failed to notice a bored Laurie slipping off the bench. She eased up beside him and planted a kiss on his ear.

Startled, he dropped the sandpaper. He grabbed her. "Want to play, huh?" He tickled her.

She squirmed, trying to get away. "Stop it." She giggled.

"Sorry to interrupt." Margaret stood at the foot of the stairs with Sobra beside her. Wrapped in a heavy blue housecoat, her face and eyes puffy with cold, Margaret looked worried.

Dan asked, "What's wrong?"

Holding a tissue to her nose with one hand, Margaret patted the black Labrador with the other.

"Sobra here woke me up. She heard a noise coming from the Wilson's house next door."

Laurie was instantly alert. "Aren't the Wilsons vacationing in Florida?"

"That's right. There's a light moving around inside the house, as if someone was searching it with a flashlight. I've called the police. They should be here any minute. The Wilsons left me a key for the front door of their house. Dan, I told the police you'd give it to them. You're to meet them at the north end of the alley where you can't be seen from the Wilson's house. The police want to catch the intruders in the act, if they can."

Dan headed for the stairway. "I'll get my coat."

A few minutes later Dan was back in Margaret's kitchen, where he found the two women sitting at the table in the dark. He shivered. "It's freezing out there and I forgot my gloves." He blew on his cupped hands. "Why didn't you turn on a light?"

Margaret answered. "We thought it might alert the robber or distract the police."

"Good thinking. Sergeant Beacon said to stay in the house until everything is over. There are at least two squad cars out there." He joined them at the kitchen table.

They sat in silence, straining to catch any sound giving them a clue to what was happening. Once they heard shouts and the sound of running. Sobra started to bark. Margaret hushed her. It grew quiet again. Sobra curled up on the floor to sleep. The only noises were of Margaret coughing and blowing her nose. Time crept by with agonizing slowness in the dark. Someone knocked at the kitchen door so unexpectedly they all jumped. Sobra barked. Dan peeked out, then turned on the backyard light.

Sergeant Beacon's big frame filled the doorway, bringing a blast of frigid February air with him. Mindful of her cold, Margaret motioned for the sergeant to come on in and shut the door. Dan switched on the kitchen light.

The sergeant said, "We caught one of them in the house. Other officers are chasing the second one. I'm positive they'll catch up with him." He looked at Margaret. "Do you have an address or phone number where the Wilsons can be reached?"

"Yes, I'll get it for you."

Beacon took the slip of paper, thanked her, and then turned to Dan. "Could you come with me for a few minutes?"

"Sure." Dan followed him to the Wilson's backyard. Their backlight was on. Broken glass glistened on the steps. The top of the storm door was broken out.

Beacon pointed to the broken door. "Do you have anything we can cover that with?"

Dan put his hands under his armpits to keep them warm. "I think there's a piece of scrap plywood in Margaret's garage that should fit it. Is that how they got in?"

"Yes. They broke the glass, reached in, and unlocked the storm door. Then they jimmied the lock on the inside door."

The biting wind made Dan huddle deeper into his coat. "It must have been the sound of breaking glass that alerted Sobra, causing her to wake-up Margaret."

"Sobra!" Bill Saxon stood handcuffed and flanked on each side by a policeman. Hate twisted his mouth. "That damn dog."

One of the flanking officers jerked Bill. "That's enough."

The second officer handed Sergeant Beacon a pillowcase. "When he realized we were going to catch him, he threw this away."

Beacon searched it. It held silverware, jewelry, blank checks, two department store credit cards, and various other items. The sergeant handed the case back. "Take the evidence and suspect to headquarters. I'll be along as soon as we secure the premises."

On a warm Saturday afternoon the following mid-April, Dan was in the alley washing Margaret's old, green Buick. The garage door was up. Margaret swept the floor while Sobra lay nearby. It was a beautiful day. Margaret stopped frequently to take a deep breath, enjoying the vibes of spring. She smiled at a squirrel scampering across the telephone line. Then she glanced at Dan and frowned. "It's not necessary for you to wash my car you know. Our agreement has always been that the service station I've been dealing with for over twenty years would continue to care for it."

"I know. But I wouldn't feel right borrowing it for a date without doing something in exchange. Just putting gas in it isn't enough."

"You're like family. You don't need to repay me. I'm happy to lend you and Laurie my car."

Dan frowned as he wrung the chamois out. "I know." He slapped the chamois, harder than necessary, on the hood. "But I feel more comfortable keeping it a business arrangement."

Margaret started to reply, sighed instead, and went back to her sweeping. Dan was wringing the chamois out again when Sergeant Beacon came around the corner of the garage. The officer was dressed in casual clothes.

Margaret halted her sweeping. "Hello, Sergeant. Have you gone undercover? Or is this a social call?"

"A mixture. It's my day off, but I wanted to warn you and your neighbors to keep an eye on your pets. They released Bill Saxon yesterday."

Dan leaned against the car. "I thought he couldn't raise the bail money."

"He talked his mother into mortgaging her house with a disreputable loan company."

Margaret said, "Poor woman. That's bound to give her financial grief on top of everything else she has to bear."

Dan asked, "When is Bill's court date?"

"His lawyer managed to get it delayed until late July."

"He'll be running free till then?"

"That's right. And he's mad. He knows this time he's going to prison for sure." The sergeant glanced down at Sobra who cautiously smelled him over. Beacon reached out to pet her. She jumped back.

Margaret said, "Sobra is skittish around people she doesn't know well. It frightens her when they make sudden moves towards her."

"I see." The big, dark man crouched down to Sobra's level and extended his hand palm up. He held still, letting Sobra check him over on her own terms. Thanks to his approach she soon warmed up to him and enjoyed a good petting.

Beacon glanced up at Margaret. "If I were you, I would keep an extra good eye on your pets, especially Sobra here." He gave the black Lab one last pat and stood up. "If my guess in right, Bill's out to get revenge for getting caught. And he doesn't care what he takes it out on."

A lump rose in Dan's throat. The image of Bill, dripping white paint, threatening to kill him, flashed before his eyes. "Can't you." He tried to clear his throat. "Can't you do anything, Sergeant Beacon?"

"You can't arrest a man because you suspect he's up to no good. He has to actually do something that is provable." He said apologetically, "My threatening him won't work anymore. He's too angry to care."

Dan felt sick to his stomach and ashamed at the same time for being afraid. "What can a man do to protect himself?"

"Oh, you don't have to worry. Bill's not going to risk adding to his prison term by going after people. He'll take it out on those least protected by law—the animals."

He pointed to Sobra. "He blames her in particular for getting caught."

Dan breathed a sigh of relief. Margaret said, "Thank you for warning us, Sergeant Beacon. I promise we will take precautions."

"Good." He shifted nervously, as if hesitant to speak.

Margaret asked, "Is there something else on your mind, Sergeant?"

He shuffled his big feet in embarrassment. "Well, we have only known each other on a very casual basis. And I wouldn't blame you for not wanting to discuss it with me. You might think it is too personal." He stopped, reluctant to go on.

Margaret smiled reassuringly. "You want to ask me something?"

"Yes."

"About my gift?"

Beacon grinned, relieved. "Yes, Madam, if you don't mind."

"What specifically did you want to know, Sergeant?"

"Well. I've wondered for a long time." He hesitated, then blurted out, "Do you have any idea why you possess an ability others don't?"

Margaret smiled warmly. "Sergeant, I have asked myself that same question many times over the years. I really don't know the answer. However, I have formed some opinions based on what I've observed. For more years than I care to remember, I have studied people as they discussed and interacted with animals. I've noticed there is one big difference between them and myself. It has to do with attitude."

"What kind of attitude?"

"Equal but different."

"I beg your pardon?"

"Every person I know, including those who deeply love animals, consider themselves superior to animals. I don't. I believe animals are equal but different. Like apples or oranges, or men and women. The same life force, or energy, flows through animal, plant, and man, and that life force is a part of God. Therefore, I think the American Indian was on the right track when he called an animal brother."

Dan flared. "That's ridiculous. Everyone knows man is superior to animals."

"In what way?"

Dan hesitated. What was he getting himself into? Then he realized that, with graduation so close, he no longer had to worry about losing his room and board. He was finally free to challenge Margaret and, hopefully, expose the evil behind her gift. He smiled as he answered, "In brain power."

"I'll agree man does have greater reasoning capabilities. He needs them to be creative. God created man in His own image. God, being the Creator, formed a creature capable of creating through his thoughts. Man was also given a body form that enables him to make what he imagines in his mind."

Pleased with himself for scoring a point, Dan added. "Man is more dexterous all the way around."

"Is he more agile that a monkey?"

"Well. No. Not entirely."

"Is he quicker than a panther?"

"No."

"Does he possess greater smelling capabilities than a bloodhound?"

"No."

"Better eyesight than a bird of prey?"

"No."

"Then you base your claim that man is superior on one characteristic—his brain power, as you put it. Isn't that like saying a bee is better than a cow because it creates honey instead of milk?"

"But people have feelings."

"So do animals. Just observe how happy a dog is when greeting its master, or how disturbed it is when scolded by that same master. Animals just don't continue to hang on to feelings like man does. But man and animal share a common foundation of physical and emotional sensations."

"But man was given dominion over the earth."

Margaret smiled. "Is the president of a corporation superior to his employees? Or simply more powerful because of his position?"

"He has to have some sort of superior ability to be a successful president."

"Granted. He needs good managerial skills. Are his talents really superior to those of the skilled craftsman he hires? Or merely different? Do the reasoning abilities that qualify man to dominate the earth make him superior? Or just differently skilled?

Before Dan could reply, Sergeant Beacon shot him a look, elegantly communicating his disapproval of Dan's disrespectful tone. Dan decided to drop the subject. He wasn't getting anywhere anyway.

The police officer turned to Margaret. "If this attitude of equal though different holds the key to communicating psychically with animals, how does it work?"

"First, you must realize that man, animal, plant, and earth were created from, and with, the same fundamental energies. This kinship gives all life forms a common psychic bond at that energy level. It is an intuitive level. And it is what enables animals to sense their owners moods and thoughts, and respond accordingly. As with any of the senses, some are more adept at doing that than others."

"How does man fit into the picture?"

"It is man's ignorance of our universal connectivity, and resulting attitudes of superiority, that blocks his ability to understand animals. When an animal is approached from an attitude of equal but different, and with respect for it as an individual, I believe the barriers start to fall. And the deeper the love bond that exists between man and animal, the greater the possibility of psychic connection with the animal. Because that fundamental energy is love."

Beacon mulled over her words. "Do you think anyone can develop your ability if they learned to respect animals the way you do?"

"I don't know. But I think it's a possibility. I must warn you though. It isn't as easy as it sounds. You can't just believe it intellectually. You must be convinced to the very core of your being because that is where the psychic connection exists. Man has had centuries to develop his feelings of superiority. Regardless of their sincerity, and how hard they try, some could find it impossible to overcome such deeply ingrained programming."

Dan couldn't stand it. He had to try again. He had to win a point. He blurted out. "The Bible says God told man to subdue the earth."

Margaret chuckled. "Who has the greater subduing success? The one who controls only outward behavior through power and manipulation; or the one who controls the heart because he has learned to be at one with it, through love and respect? Which method do you think would best meet God's approval?"

Dan glared at her. This woman was impossible. No matter what you say, she always has a comeback. Wanting a way out, he looked at his watch. "It's getting late." He picked his chamois up off the Buick's hood. "I have to get back to work so I can have time to get ready for my date."

Sergeant Beacon glanced at his watch. "I've got to get going too. Would you mind, Mrs. Canfield, warning your neighbors about the threat to their pets?"

Margaret leaned her broom against the wall. "Of course not. I'll put Sobra in the house and get started right away."

Dan didn't even bother to look up when they left. He angrily scrubbed a back tire. What nonsense. Everyone knows man is superior to animals and that animals were only created for man's use. An unwelcome thought flitted through his mind. Who is everyone? Isn't it man himself? How reliable is the judgment of someone with as big an ego as man? Dan attacked the tire as if he was trying to rub a hole right through it—and Margaret's ideas.

CHAPTER TEN

Four days before graduation Dan and Laurie left after an early showing at the local movie theater and drove to a secluded area where they parked. They snuggled close and kissed, stoking the fires already burning brightly in both.

Reluctantly, Dan pulled back. "We can't afford to get carried away, Laurie. There's something we need to talk about."

"What?" She nuzzled a spot behind his ear.

He squirmed. "Quit that. You know what it does to me." She tired to nuzzle his ear again. He dodged. "Look, we don't have a lot of time." He gave her a peck on the nose. "In order to keep the car, I had to promise to pick Margaret up later this evening. Someone called her at the last minute to act as a substitute speaker at a Church Women United meeting. There wasn't time to make other transportation arrangements."

Laurie sighed. "Okay." She snuggled down into his shoulder. "What is it?"

"I got a phone call today. How does the first Saturday in August sound for our wedding?"

Laurie gasped and balanced off his shoulder. "You've got a job!"

Dan grinned. "Starting a week from Monday."

Laurie hugged Dan so hard it felt like she was trying to squeeze through him. "Where?"

"In the sales department of a tool company in Indianapolis. They make hand tools for craftsman and hobbyists. It was my experience as a handyman that cinched it. They said they wanted someone with business training that had a working knowledge of their consumers' needs."

"That's great. But won't you need a car?"

"I have enough left in my savings to make a small down payment on a used one. Want to come along tomorrow to help me pick it out?"

She kissed his cheek. "Try and stop me."

"There's just one thing."

"What's that?"

"You haven't said the first Saturday in August is okay for our wedding."

"Oh, Dan. It's more than okay. It's perfect." She gave him a kiss that erased all memory of his promise to pick up Margaret. She pulled her lips away before he was ready. She said excitedly. "Let's go."

"What's your hurry?" He pulled her close for another kiss.

She put her hand on his chest. "I want to go tell my family. And Margaret." She laughed. "I want to tell the whole world."

Dan gave her cheek a series of pecks, each time moving closer to her lips. "There's no hurry." He started to kiss her fully on the mouth.

She pulled away. "I'm too excited to wait. Maybe Margaret's meeting has ended early. Let's go see."

Dan sighed. "Okay. I know when to give up."

The lovers slipped quietly into an empty back pew of the United Methodist Church. Women of all ages and creeds, representing a variety of local churches, filled the front of the sanctuary. Margaret stood, impeccably groomed in a blue suit, at ease behind the lectern. She flipped a note card over. "That concludes my presentation about the work of the shelter." Her eyes swept the audience. "Are there any questions?"

An elderly woman raised her hand. "What do you see as the ultimate answer to the pet overpopulation problem?"

"The awakening of every pet owner who lets their pets breed indiscriminately that he or she is partly responsible for the misery and/or destruction of thousands of puppies and kittens each year. The ultimate solution lies with people choosing to raise their consciousness and not with the animal welfare organizations they shove their responsibilities onto."

A middle-aged woman raised her hand. "I assume you know everyone here was expecting to hear a missionary from Africa. I'll admit your talk was interesting. But there are starving children in the world. And souls that need saving. After all, an animal is an animal. It has no soul. Don't you think we should limit our concerns to humans?"

Margaret stiffened.

"Oh, oh," Laurie whispered to Dan. "That lady just hit a sore spot with Margaret."

With her best intimidating, monarchical look, Margaret answered sharply. "Compassion and love should know no boundaries." She caught herself and smiled at her questioner. She took in the woman's lack of make-up, hair in a bun, and plain brown dress. "You appear to be a woman who takes her religion seriously. I would guess you can quote the Bible backwards and forwards." Encouraged by the nodding of heads surrounding the woman, Margaret continued. "Can you tell me what were the first responsibilities God gave man and woman?"

As the woman tried to think, Dan leaned forward. At last, he thought, here was someone who might be a match for Margaret. Someone capable of breaking through her pleasant façade and revealing the truth about the evil behind it.

The woman's face lit up as she remembered. She rose and in a lordly voice said, "Genesis 1:28. 'And God blessed them, and God said unto them, Be fruitful, and multiply, and replenish the earth, and subdue it: and have dominion over the fish of the sea, and over the fowl of the air, and over every living thing that moveth upon the earth.'" She looked proudly around the audience. "That's the King James Version of course."

"Very good. Thank you. Now correct me if I'm wrong. But doesn't your particular church teach that there is a literal judgment day where God is going to judge every Christian on how well he or she kept His commandants?"

"That's right."

"I'm sure you would agree that the ruler of a domain can be insensitive, caring nothing for the physical or emotional needs of those he rules. Or he can be compassionate and loving, putting the welfare of his subjects above his own interests. Isn't that true?"

"I suppose so. Yes."

"Which type would you say God wants man to be?"

The woman shrugged. "Compassionate and loving."

"Then, if there is a literal judgment day, as you believe, isn't it reasonable to expect Him to judge the way we handle the very first commandant God gave man? How well has man cared for the earth and its creatures and subdued—that is controlled—them for the mutual benefit of both?" The woman looked uncomfortable. She sat down without answering.

Dan leaned back, disappointed. Another woman, who looked the stereotypical farmer's wife, raised her hand. He leaned forward again when she asked, "Are you saying it's wrong to kill animals?"

"For ego-gratification, greed, or sheer pleasure, yes it's wrong. To meet genuine needs for food and clothing, I honestly don't know. Nature is so designed that life must feed upon life. Whether it is a carrot or a cow, one life form must be consumed that another might be sustained. I am sure, however, that while death means little to animals, emotional and physical pain does. The main issue, therefore, is how we respect and handle each living entity, carrot or cow, up to and including the moment of use."

An attractive woman near the back held up her hand. She motioned toward the woman in the brown dress, who had spoken earlier. "Unlike her church, our religion doesn't see God as a punishing God. He is a forgiving Father who asks only that we believe in Jesus. We do not believe in a literal judgment day for Christians."

"But you do believe in honoring God?"

"Of course."

"How can man be honoring God if he is dishonoring His creation?"

"What?"

"Are you showing respect for the artist when you misuse his creations?"

"I never thought about it before."

"Considering what man is doing to this earth, himself, and other life forms, perhaps it's time we all thought about it." Margaret's eyes swept the audience, a challenge in her expression. "How can we claim to be true Christians as long as we abuse what God so lovingly entrusted to our care? Hasn't it ever occurred to any of you that God and *all* his creations are so intertwined—so at one—that any mistreatment of the created touches the Creator?"

A low murmur raced through the crowd. Neighbor consulted neighbor. No one answered Margaret. She calmly waited.

A woman sitting in the front row stood up and looked around. She stepped up on the platform, next to Margaret. In a loud voice, the woman asked, "Are there any more questions?" The audience quieted, but said nothing. After a reasonable wait, she turned to

Margaret. "We thank you for your interesting and -ah- challenging talk. We'll be breaking for refreshments soon. You are welcome to stay and partake with us."

"Thank you. But I see my ride is here. I have to go." Margaret left the platform accompanied by muted, uncertain applause.

Dan and Laurie followed her out of the sanctuary and into the hallway. Margaret smiled weakly at Laurie. "I'm afraid I got carried away. I hadn't planned to speak on anything but the shelter's work. I may have alienated the very support I had hoped to gain by agreeing to speak here. I was too blunt."

Laurie put an arm around her. "You presented the truth as you saw it. Didn't you?"

"Yes."

"Then don't worry about it. You have always told me it was best to be honest with people about how you felt. Then leave the rest in God's hands. He knows what's going on in their hearts better than you."

Margaret chuckled. "It's disconcerting to have your own advice thrown back at you. But you're right. I'll try not to let it worry me."

"Good. Besides Dan and I have some news that will cheer you up." She filled Margaret in as they left the church and headed for the car.

A disappointed Dan trailed behind, rehashing Margaret's conversation with the audience. He had hoped one of those women would be able to come back at Margaret in a way that would break through her aura of authority to its source. The problem was she kept throwing out ideas her listeners had never considered. Honoring God had to include reverence for all life or it wasn't complete? Man might be held accountable for his treatment of nature and animals? How can you think of a comeback when you are still reeling from hearing such startling ideas?

Barely aware of Laurie and Margaret deep in conversation ahead of him, he trudged through the dark parking lot. Thank God he would soon be rid of Margaret. While he had hoped to see, before he moved, some sort of evidence that her gift was as evil as he had been taught, he was still glad that his life with her would soon be a repressed memory. He planned to move out right after the graduation ceremony. He took a deep breath. The very thought made him feel free already.

Still talking, the women stood by the car, waiting for him. As he fumbled in his pocket for the keys, Laurie exclaimed to Margaret, "That's a great idea." She turned excitedly to Dan. "Margaret has offered to let you live with her rent free until our wedding."

"What!"

"It makes sense doesn't it? If you move back to your parents as you planned, you'll be almost two hours from both your job and me. Here you'll only be an hour from work."

Dan's fleeting sense of freedom disappeared. "Yes, but…"

"You agreed it was silly to sign a lease on an apartment or house until I found a teaching position. Wherever we pick should be as convenient to both jobs as possible."

"I know, but…"

"And we can use the money you save to help buy furniture and pay for the wedding."

"Yes, but..."

Margaret added, "If you're worried about being beholden to me, don't. I'm sure we can figure out something for you to do in your spare time that will ease your conscience."

Dan felt the trap closing. "Yes, but..."

Laurie threw up her hands. "But what?"

Dan racked his brain trying to come up with a reason to say no. There were none that wouldn't result in an argument with Laurie. "Nothing. It's not important."

He sighed. "You're right. I guess." He looked at Margaret. "It's only on condition I can earn my keep like always."

"Agreed."

Laurie gave Dan a peck on the cheek. "Now that that's settled, let's go tell my parents the good news. Margaret, you come over to. I know Mom wants your input."

Laurie's mother was as excited as Laurie was. Motioning for Margaret and Laurie to sit down at her kitchen table, she left the room. Returning with an armful of bridal magazines, she said, "I know it's getting late, but I want to discuss wedding plans." She plopped the magazines on the table, sank into a chair, and looked up at the still standing men. "Frank, you and Dan go visit in the living room. This is woman's talk."

Startled, Dan said, "But--but it's my wedding too."

Frank slapped him on the back. "Come on, Son. You and Laurie will have plenty of opportunities to discuss marriage plans together. I want to hear about your new job."

Laurie added, "Don't worry, Dan. No decisions will be made without your approval. Mom knows it wouldn't be right." Catherine nodded in agreement.

Reassured, Dan let Frank lead him into the living room. The evening was warm. A gentle breeze floated through the open windows. Eager to talk about his job, Dan and Frank were soon engrossed in conversation. An hour and half flew by without them noticing. Dan was vaguely aware a dog had started barking somewhere, but he paid no attention.

Suddenly, Margaret barged through the door, followed by the Carpenter women. "Sobra's barking from inside my house." She glanced from Frank to Dan. "I think someone is sneaking around it."

The two men leaped to their feet. Frank disappeared into their bedroom. He returned carrying a large black flashlight and an old wooden baseball bat. He handed Dan the bat. Holding the flashlight like a weapon, he said, "Ready Son? Let's go out the front and circle around. Whoever is there is probably in the back where he can't be seen from the street." He turned to the women. "One of you call the police."

Frank opened the front door quietly. He murmured to Dan, "Our porch has a couple of squeaky boards. So step where I step. We don't want to inadvertently warn whoever it is." In single file, they tiptoed across the porch. The sky was clear and moon full. Frank leaned his head close to Dan and whispered, "There's enough light without using the flashlight." Dan nodded.

With Frank still leading, they slipped off the porch and crept around the corner of the house. Dan could feel his heart beating in his ears. His sweating hands gripped the worn bat tighter. He prayed the intruder was alone, and wouldn't put up a fight. Sobra still barked frantically from inside Margaret's darkened house.

Dan was close on Frank's heels when, suddenly, the older man pitched forward. His flashlight struck their aluminum siding. Dan sidestepped to keep from falling on the downed man. Frank blurted, "Damn. I tripped over our garden hose."

A figure bolted across Margaret's backyard, toward her back gate. Frank yelled, "Go after him, Dan."

But Dan was already running. He sped through the Carpenter's yard, around Margaret's garage, to her open gate. He stood panting, looking left and right, front and back. The intruder had disappeared. He returned to find Frank getting to his feet. Breathless, Dan asked, "Are you all right?"

"Yes. Just mad at myself for leaving the hose out." He kicked at the hose, lying like a snake in the shadowy grass. "I'm getting as careless as a kid." He grabbed up his flashlight. "Did you see who it was?"

"No. He was gone by the time I got there."

Disappointed, Frank said, "Let's go tell the women."

Twenty minutes later, Margaret's back light was on, Sobra had calmed down, and the police were searching the area. Dan stood in the backyard with Margaret and the three Carpenters. A large wooden box sat upside-down under Margaret's open kitchen window. The screen had a hole cut in it a little larger than a man's fist.

Laurie snuggled against Dan. He put his arm around her. She asked, "Why would anyone make a hole that size?"

"I think I can answer that." Sergeant Beacon had come up the walk behind them. He held a meat wrapper. He opened it, showing them a hamburger patty. "I found this down the alley. My guess is the lab will find it contains poison."

The five civilians said in unison, "Poison!"

"That's right. He wasn't trying to break in. He only wanted to make an opening big enough to toss this meat to the dog. Judging from the evidence, he must have been ready to throw it in when you scared him off."

Margaret sank down on her back step. She said sadly, "Bill Saxon."

Beacon said, "That's the way I figure it. He still wants revenge for getting caught burglarizing the Wilson's home. The neighborhood has been keeping too close a tab on their pets, frustrating him. He knows he only has till his court date. The more his efforts are blocked, the bolder he gets. Otherwise, he never would have risked doing this with lights on in the house next door. Unfortunately, there isn't enough proof that he's the culprit to arrest him."

Dan said, "He is really sick. A real mental case."

Margaret sighed. "In spite of all he's done, I still can't help remembering Bill as a little boy. Blast his father anyway. And blast Bill for not admitting he has a problem and getting help." She glanced up at Beacon. "You know Bill is not going to give up trying as long as he's free. What can I do to protect Sobra and my cats?"

"I really don't know Mrs. Canfield. Never letting them out of your sight when they're outdoors and never leaving them alone in the house is all I can suggest. I realize that's impractical. The only alternative is to install an elaborate alarm system."

"I can't afford that."

"I didn't think you could. Most people can't."

Dan squeezed Laurie. He whispered in her ear, "I just figured out how I can earn part of my keep for the next couple of months."

"How?"

"I'm going to do some research and see if I can figure out a way to make Margaret an alarm system."

On a cloudy night, three weeks later, Margaret and Dan were gone. Someone cut through the clear fishing line Dan had weaved through the window screens. It set off a bell that woke the whole neighborhood. After Frank shut the alarm off, he found a hamburger patty in the grass.

CHAPTER ELEVEN

The first evening in July was mild. A soft breeze flowed through the open kitchen window, caressing Dan as he sharpened Margaret's kitchen knives. Margaret stood at the back door, keeping an eye on Sobra, who was doing her business in the backyard. The doorbell rang, causing the sleeping Princess to jump and fall off the chair she was curled up on.

Dan laid the knife and sharpener down. "I'll get it. It's probably Laurie. She should be home from her summer job at the park." Still chuckling over Princess's startled reaction, he opened the front door.

An excited Laurie waved a note in his face. With dark eyes sparkling, she said, "I've got a teaching job."

"You do!" He grabbed her, planting a kiss. "Where?"

"Right here in town. Where I did my student teaching. The home economics teacher's husband is being transferred out of state. She recommended me to replace her."

Dan twirled her so fast that Taylor, who had accompanied him to the door, ran for cover. Laurie squealed, "Stop it, Dan! You're making me dizzy."

He laughed, then halted. He grasped her shoulders, searching her face. "You know what this means don't you?"

She said teasingly, "What?"

"It means we can get a place now." He cast his arms heavenward. "I can move."

He grabbed her shoulders again. "It ought to be halfway between here and Indianapolis. Then neither of us will have over a thirty minute drive." He hugged her. "This is great."

"What's all the excitement?" Margaret appeared in the hallway. "I could feel it all the way to the back door."

Laurie raced to her and gave her a squeeze. "I've got a job."

Margaret's smile weakened. "That's nice." Sadness appeared in her gray-green eyes. "I'm glad for you."

Puzzled, Laurie eyed her. "What's the matter, Margaret? Aren't you happy for us?"

"Of course. It's just--well--I'm going to miss having Dan around. I'm even going to miss you running in and out like a friendly puppy."

Laurie laughed. "You're not getting rid of us that easy. With Mom and Dad living next door, there will be plenty of opportunities to see us again." She glanced at Dan. "Isn't that right, Dan?"

Dan wasn't thrilled at the thought. It never occurred to him that Margaret could still be a part of his life after he moved. He swallowed his misgivings and nodded. "That's right."

Margaret smiled at him. "But it won't be the same, Dan. It meant a great deal to me to have you here. More than you'll ever know." He was too embarrassed to reply. She continued. "I only wish I could come up with an appropriate wedding gift for you. One that would express my special love for both of you."

Laurie hugged her. "Are you still concerned about that? Don't fret so much. Anything you pick will be fine." She halted. "Isn't that Sobra barking?"

"Oh dear. I was so distracted by your excited voices, I completely forgot Sobra was still in the backyard. I'd better go get her."

Laurie frowned. "You'd better hurry. Bill was outdoors in his yard when I arrived. He could have seen her. She might be barking at him."

Margaret rushed off. Laurie started to follow her, but Dan clutched her arm. "Margaret can handle it." He pulled her close, kissing her dimpled cheek. "You and I have some plans to discuss."

He started to kiss her on the mouth, but was stopped midway by the sound of Margaret screaming, "No! No!" There was a loud blast, followed in a split-second by a second blast.

Dan stood rooted with his arms still around Laurie. "That was a shotgun."

The color drained from Laurie's face. "Oh, my God. Bill!" They raced to the back door.

The yard light flooded the night scene with a yellow glow. Margaret was lying on the sidewalk. She was covered with blood from a wound in her abdomen. She squirmed, trying to reach Sobra who was lying in the grass an arm's length away. She too was covered with blood. Margaret called weakly, "Sobra." The Labrador whimpered and tried to wag her tail. Margaret struggled to get up.

Laurie and Dan dropped down on each side of her. They gently forced her back. Laurie said, "Don't move. Oh, God. Please don't move."

Margaret coughed. A thin line of blood trickled from the corner of her mouth. "Sobra's hurt. She needs me."

Dan held her down. "You're hurt too. You mustn't move. You'll aggravate your injuries." He heard the sound of running feet and a gate opening. Laurie's parents rushed over.

Catherine gasped, "My God." She ran into Margaret's house, yelling over her shoulder, "I'll call an ambulance."

Frank said, "I'll get some blankets to cover her." He raced back to his house.

Sobra whined. Margaret fought Laurie and Dan's efforts to hold her down. "Sobra needs help." Too weak, she fell back. "Someone please help Sobra."

Dan shifted to the Labrador. Not knowing what else to do, he gently stroked her head. Sobra wagged her tail feebly and stared straight ahead. An enormous lump rose in Dan's throat. He fought back tears threatening to spill from his eyes. How could anyone do this? Suddenly he was aware of someone coming up the sidewalk.

Bill Saxon stopped at Margaret's feet. The butt of his shotgun dragged the ground. All his cockiness was gone. He pointed a shaky finger at Margaret. "You shouldn't have moved in front of the dog like that. I didn't want to hurt you. But I couldn't help it." He wailed, "It was the dog I was after. Just the dog."

Dan jumped up with fists clenched. He didn't care if Bill was bigger and a more experienced fighter. He was going to pound that pleading face until it looked like Margaret's belly. He took a step towards the big, starchless man.

Margaret cried feebly, "Dan, don't." He stopped and glared at her. The trickle of blood from her mouth had widened. She coughed. "Revenge won't help."

Dan lashed out angrily. "How can you say that after what he's done to Sobra and you?"

"It wasn't Sobra he really wanted to hurt."

Bill looked startled. "What?"

Margaret flinched in pain. "For once be man enough to see the truth, Bill. Every time you've hurt an animal, it was really your father you were trying to hurt."

Bill dropped the shotgun. He sank slowly to his knees, buried his face in his hands, and moaned.

Dan stared at the wilted man in amazement. Margaret's words had also struck a cord in him. He suddenly realized that brawn and fearlessness were not what made a man. No, the true man was the one who had learned to know, and control himself. With that realization, Dan's insecurity about his manhood disappeared for good.

Catherine popped out of the back door. "The ambulance and police are on their way." Her words brought them all back to the immediate problem.

Margaret tried to grasp Laurie's arm. "Tell Catherine to call the vet. Sobra needs help too." She glanced at Dan. "Promise me you'll take her to him." She coughed harshly.

Tears again welled up in his eyes. "I'll take her."

Laurie yelled, "Call the vet!"

Catherine disappeared inside as Frank arrived with some old army blankets. He and Laurie tried to cover Margaret. In a weakening voice, she said, "No." She tried to pull the blanket off. "Sobra's in shock. She needs the blanket."

Frank patted her shoulder. "Don't worry, Margaret. I brought enough for both of you."

Margaret silently watched Dan and Frank wrap Sobra in a blanket. In spite of their best efforts to be gentle, the dog yelped in pain. Margaret's eyes glistened with tears. In a voice barely audible, she said, "Poor Sobra. I tried so hard to help her overcome her fears. What's going to happen to her now?"

Laurie squeezed her hand. "Margaret, please don't talk. You need to save your strength."

Catherine came out of the house. Sizing up the situation, she slipped up to Dan. She whispered, "Margaret's not going to keep still until she knows Sobra is on her way to the vet. You take the dog now. There is nothing you can do here anyway, and the vet is waiting."

Overhearing her, Frank added, "I'll help you load Sobra in the car. I've got a piece of wood we can slip under her to keep from aggravating her injuries."

Dan nodded in agreement. While he waited beside Sobra for Frank to get the board, he glanced around. Regardless of how long he lived, he knew he would never get the scene out of his mind. The clear, mild evening. The far off sound of sirens growing closer. The yard light bathing everything with a yellow glow. Crickets singing in the dark. Bill moaning at Margaret's feet, and Laurie clutching her hand. Blood splattered on the sidewalk and grass, sprinkled in Margaret's beauty parlor hairdo, and beginning to seep through the blankets that covered Sobra and Margaret. It would be the blood he would remember most.

Knowing it would be what Margaret wanted, Dan stayed at the animal clinic until he learned how Sobra's surgery went. Then he headed for the hospital. Laurie and her parents were the only ones in the waiting room. Laurie's tan slacks were stained with dried blood and grass. She dashed into his arms.

He brushed a lock of hair off her forehead. "How's Margaret?"

She shook her head. "She's out of surgery, but it doesn't look good. The doctor told us to call her son in California. He won't be able to get a plane until tomorrow."

Her chin quivered. "It's so hard to believe. One minute we're all happy and excited. In the next, Margaret is dying." She burst into tears. "I just can't understand it."

He held her, letting her soak his shirt with her tears. He fought back his own urge to cry. Margaret didn't deserve this. Sure she had a suspicious gift and he had refused to trust or like her because of it. But neither she nor Sobra deserved to be shot down like rabid animals.

Frank cleared his throat. "How's Sobra?"

"She'll live. She's going to have a permanent limp due to some damage to her hip. Otherwise, she'll be fine."

Catherine brightened. "That's wonderful. Knowing Sobra's going to be all right just may give Margaret the edge she needs to keep fighting."

A male voice said, "I'm afraid that probably won't be enough." The doctor stood in the doorway and continued. "I'm sorry. But the damage is too extensive and she wouldn't allow us to put her on life support. I doubt that she lasts till morning." His sad eyes swept over the seated older couple, holding hands, and the standing young couple, clinging to each other. "I'm sorry. Which of you are Dan and Laurie?"

Dan answered, "We are."

"She's semiconscious and asking for you."

"Does she know how bad her condition is?"

"She knows. He shook his head in wonderment. "She told me not too feel bad. That she didn't mind, in the least, crossing over to the other side. She is really something else."

Margaret's eyes were closed when Dan and Laurie entered her room. The head of her bed was raised slightly. Tubes ran from various parts of her body to bottles and bags. Machines worked impersonally checking her condition and easing her breathing. Laurie and Dan tiptoed to the bed, positioning themselves on each side. Margaret opened her eyes. She said something too low to hear. Dan and Laurie each took a cold hand and leaned forward to catch her words. She repeated, "How's Sobra?"

Dan responded, "She's going to make it."

Tears dropped out of the corners of Margaret's eyes. She spoke with a voice they had to strain to hear. "Poor Sobra. All my efforts will be undone." She coughed weakly. "A stranger won't know how to handle her, even if she's lucky enough to find a new owner."

Laurie said, "Margaret, I have an idea. You know the wedding gift you've worried about getting us?"

Dan flared. "Laurie! Now's not the time to...." Margaret stopped him with a feeble motion and indicated she wanted to hear what Laurie had to say.

Laurie continued. "We've watched you turn a high-strung, fearful dog into an obedient, loving companion. How could anything reflect your special brand of love better than Sobra?"

Dan smiled admiringly at Laurie. "That's a great idea." He squeezed Margaret's cold hand. "Can we have Sobra? I promise you we'll take good care of her. You've taught us how."

"Oh, yes." Her troubled expression disappeared. "Oh, yes." She whispered, "Bless you both." A peace settled over her and she closed her eyes.

Dan glanced at Laurie. "Maybe we'd better go."

Margaret's eyes fluttered open. She mouthed, "Stay. You, Frank and Catherine. I don't want to be alone." She slipped into a coma shortly after greeting

Laurie's parents. The two couples sat with her through the long night. Her body functions ceased one by one, and her heart ended its last beat—just as the dawn broke.

EPILOGUE

The seasons moved through their cycles. Five years passed smoothly and quickly for Dan and Laurie. Dan stood, holding a cup of coffee, on the back patio of their recently purchased home. He was proud of the way he and Laurie had managed to live on his salary while saving hers so they could buy this modest place in the country. He contentedly surveyed the fenced-in, wooded three acres that made up their backyard. The crisp, bright April morning vibrated with the rejuvenation of nature after a long, cold winter.

Dan never felt so fulfilled and at peace in his whole life. He was worn out from being up all night, but it was a good tiredness. He had just returned from witnessing the birth of their first child, named Margaret Jean Hanley at Laurie's insistence. Laurie and baby were beautiful.

He chuckled at the antics of Katy and Princess as they leaped and played at the base of a maple tree. He was glad he and Laurie had given into pressure from the shelter to take all of Margaret's pets. They had given them a lot of pleasure.

Sobra trotted, with a limp, out of the woods. She'd been exploring what was still new territory. Seeing Dan, she wagged her tail in greeting. Catching sight of something, she disappeared again into the woods. Dan smiled.

Instantly, Dan was transported out of himself. In a split-second everything was brighter—more brilliant than anything he had ever known, yet the light wasn't blinding or uncomfortable. Everything was clearer. And joyous. He felt a oneness with the trees, animals, earth—and God. For an instant he experienced all nature functioning from a continual spirit of joy and love. He felt an intelligence permeating the trees, rocks, and all seemingly inanimate and animate objects. All were manifestations of one universal spirit. He knew, without knowing how he knew that he was the trees, the grass, and the animals. That he and they were one at the core of their beings.

In a split-second, he sensed that of all earth's life forms, man is the only creature capable of blocking his own sense of oneness and is, therefore, the most spiritually dead.

Just as quickly as it came, the experience was over. Dan stood, still holding his coffee cup, with mind whirling. What happened? Had he gone insane? Was he more exhausted than he realized? Had he hallucinated? What was the lingering sense of joy and peace he still felt? What had happened!

Out of the storehouse of his memories, flashed a scene of him sitting on the front porch with Laurie and

Margaret. Margaret was telling of her experience with something that she called cosmic consciousness. She had described it as a mystical, fleeting, unexpected tuning into the universe.

He shook his head. It can't be! Then he recalled declaring to himself that he would never believe she was telling the truth unless he experienced it for himself. Dan laughed, and said aloud, "All right, Margaret." He shook his fist at the bright sky. "I know now that at least some of what you said was true."

As he stood there still reeling from his experience, he sensed the presence of someone smiling. The smile was so wide, the upper lip completely disappeared.

-End-

About The Author

Rita has been a school librarian, part-time church secretary, substitute teacher, and is currently a full time homemaker. But she considers her true vocation that of student and seeker of the hidden realities behind life and its purpose.

She has been a hospice volunteer, certified church lay speaker, member of a writers' group, and serves on the board of a homeless animal shelter. She is currently still actively learning, pursing writing, and spending time with her husband, Howard, a retired high school teacher.

They live in Shelbyville, Indiana with two dogs, three cats, and a cockatiel. She is working on her second book, *I Wonder, a Hodgepodge Reflecting upon Life.*

Printed in the United States
25216LVS00001B/86